The
Angel
of Galilea

The
Angel
of Galilea

Laura Restrepo

Translated by Dolores M. Koch

 Crown Publishers, Inc. / New York

Published by Crown Publishers, Inc., 201 East 50th Street, New York, New York 10022. Member of the Crown Publishing Group.

Random House, Inc. New York, Toronto, London, Sydney, Auckland
www.randomhouse.com

Originally published in Spanish as *Dulce compañia* by Grupo Editorial Norma, in 1995. This English translation was originally published by HarperCollins Publishers (Australia) in 1997.

CROWN and colophon are trademarks of Crown Publishers, Inc.

Design by Leonard Henderson

Printed in the United States of America

Library of Congress Cataloging-in-Publication Data
Restrepo, Laura.
[Dulce compañia. English]
The angel of Galilea / Laura Restrepo ; translated by Dolores M. Koch.—1st American ed.
I. Koch, Dolores. II. Title.
PQ84180.28.E7255D8513 1997
863—dc21 98–10704

ISBN 0-609-60326-4

10 9 8 7 6 5 4 3 2 1

First American Edition

To the girls:
Carmen, Villa, Titi,
Cristina, Clara, Gloria Ceci,
Diana, and Helena

Translator's Note

I wish to thank Maria Eugenia Villa and Jorge Muñoz for their patience, grace, and knowledge, and to Lee Paradise for his indispensable support and wonderful suggestions.
—Dolores M. Koch

I Want to Thank:

My son, Pedro.

My brother-in-law, Gonzalo Mallarino Flórez, who helped me correct the original manuscript.

All those who contributed details on the world of angels or helped with this book in many other ways: Patricia de Prima, the librarians of the Angelic Library of Rome, Ana Cristina Navarro, Monsignor Iván Marín, Kelly Velásquez, María Elvira Escallón, the Matíos, Gloria Rave, Mrs. Xiona and Mrs. Luciana, Rodrigo and María del Carmén Meza, psychiatrists Ismael Roldán, Ricardo Sánchez and Ignacio Vergara, Father Jansen of the Università Gregoriana of Rome, Amparito and her great Julio, Father Daniel Estivil of the Pontificio Instituto Orientale of Rome, lawyers Guillermo Baena and María Teresa Garcés, Jesuit Father Alejandro Angulo.

Alastair Reid, who read this novel in the air.

Thomas Colchie, who brought it down to earth.

Gonzalo Mallarino Botero, my expert head consultant.

Jesuit Father Francisco De Roux, for hours and hours of conversation.

The extraordinary and lucid Elvira Martínez.

Contents

. . . the natural weakness of women
and their sinful and acquired proclivities
to succumb to the assault of any fallen angel
have been demonstrated again.

JOSÉ SARAMAGO

Orifiel,
Angel of Light

THERE WERE NO WARNING SIGNS OF WHAT WAS ABOUT TO HAPPEN. Or maybe there were, but I was unable to interpret them. In reconstructing the sequence of events, I recall that a few days before it all started, three men raped a crazy woman in the garden in front of my building. It was around then that my neighbor's dog vaulted from a third-story window, landed on the street, and walked away unharmed. And the leper who sells lottery tickets on the corner of 92nd and 15th Streets gave birth to a healthy, beautiful baby. Surely those were signs, among many others, but then again this insane city gives off so many doomsday warnings that no one pays attention anymore. And I live in what is considered a middle-class neighborhood: one can only imagine the number of omens that crop up daily in the shantytowns.

The truth is that this story, with its supernatural echoes, which would so deeply transform my life, began at eight o'clock on a very ordinary Monday morning when, in a lousy

[1]

mood, I arrived at the editorial offices of *Somos* magazine, where I worked as a reporter. Feeling certain that my boss was about to give me a particularly loathsome assignment, I'd been dreading this moment all weekend. I was sure he would send me to cover the national beauty pageant that was getting under way in Cartagena. I was younger then, full of energy and ambition, and determined to write about things that mattered, but fate had dealt me a cruel blow, forcing me to earn my living at one of the many popular weekly tabloids.

Of all my assignments at *Somos,* covering the pageant was by far the worst. It was an unnerving task to interview thirty girls with wasp waists and wasp-size brains to match. I also have to admit that their abundant youth and trim figures wounded my pride. Even more painful was having to rhapsodize on Miss Bocayá's Pepsodent smile, Miss Tolima's dubious virginity, and Miss Arauca's preoccupation with poor children. To top it all, the beauty queens tried so hard to project a charming, naive image that they dealt with everyone on a first-name basis, kissing us, swinging their hips, bubbling over with sweetness. They even had a special name for the reporters from *Somos:* "*Sommie,* while you're interviewing me, hold my mirror so I can put on my makeup. Take this down, *Sommie:* My favorite person in the world is Mother Teresa of Calcutta." And there I'd be, standing in front of this splendid five-foot-ten figure, scribbling down streams of nonsense.

No. This year I was going to refuse to cover the pageant, even if it cost me my job. Devouring a bowl of earthworms would be preferable to being called Sommie one more time

or doing Miss Cundinamarca the favor of fetching the ear-
rings she left in the dining room. So I entered the editor's office cursing under my breath; unfortunately, I knew only too
well that it would be impossible to find another steady job
and, therefore, to resign was out of the question.

At the far side of the room I spotted the familiar bottle-
green corduroy jacket, and I thought, now the jacket will
turn around to reveal, turkey neck and all, none other than
my boss who, without greeting me, will bark out orders to
pack for Cartagena—and off goes Sommie again, having to
swallow her worms whole. The jacket turned around, and
the turkey looked at me, but contrary to my expectations, he
condescended to wish me good morning, and not a word
about Cartagena. Instead he demanded something else,
which I did not like any better.

"Get out to the Galilea district right away. An angel's been
sighted."

"What angel?"

"Whatever. I need a piece on angels."

Now Colombia happens to be the country in the world
with the most miracles per square foot. All virgins descend
from Heaven, all Christs shed tears, invisible surgeons perform appendectomies on the faithful, and soothsayers predict winning lottery numbers. This is all routine: we
maintain a direct line with the other world, and can only survive as a nation with a daily megadose of superstition. We
have always enjoyed an international monopoly on irrational
and paranormal events. And yet the editor in chief wanted a
piece on angel sightings now—not a month earlier or a

month later—merely because the topic was no longer hot in the United States.

A few months ago, the end-of-millennium and New Age winds had stirred a veritable angelic frenzy in the States. Hundreds of people had claimed to have had contact with one angel or another. Eminent scientists attested to their presence, and even the first lady, moved by the general enthusiasm, sported a brooch of cherub wings on her lapel. As usual, Americans were flogging the topic to the point of exhaustion. Eventually, the first lady dropped her wings and returned to her more classic jewelry, the scientists came back to earth, and the T-shirts printed with plump little Raphaelite angels were put on sale at half price. That signaled that it was now our turn, here in Colombia. We pick up what is already passé in Miami. Astonishing, isn't it, that we journalists spend most of our time warming up topics already cold in the United States.

Despite everything, I did not complain.

"Why the Galilea district?" I wanted to know.

"There's a woman from Galilea who comes several days a week to wash clothes for one of my wife's aunts. This woman told her about the angel. So, go out there now and get the story however you can, even if you have to make it up. And take photos, plenty of photos. Next week we'll put it on the cover."

"Can you give me a name, or an address? Any concrete details?"

"Nothing, you'll have to figure it out. What the heck do I know? When you see someone with wings, that's your angel."

Galilea. It must be one of the countless neighborhoods in the south of the city, miserable, overcrowded, devastated by gangs of youths. But its name was Galilea, and ever since I was a child, biblical names have had the power to move me. Every night before I went to bed, until I was twelve or thirteen, my grandfather used to read me a passage from the Old Testament or the Gospels. I listened, mesmerized, without understanding much but lulled by the whir of his *r*'s, which, as an old Belgian, he could never pronounce well in Spanish.

My grandfather would fall asleep halfway through his recitation, and I, entranced, would then repeat fragments from his evocative reading: Samaria, Galilee, Jacob, Rachel, Wedding at Cana, Sea of Tiberias, Mary Magdalene, Esau, Gethsemane, and the whole litany of names, ancient and mysterious, would waft its way through my bedroom in the darkness. Some words were terrifying and presaged destruction, like Mane, Thecel, and Phares, though I still do not know what they mean; others sounded incredibly harsh, like *noli me tangere*, which was what Jesus said to Mary Magdalene after his resurrection.

Even today, biblical names seem like talismans for me. Though I must admit that despite my grandfather's readings, and my own baptism and Christian upbringing, I was not a practicing Christian, perhaps not even a believer. And that is still the case: I must stress this from the outset so that nobody will be thinking, let alone hoping, that this is the story of a religious conversion.

I confess that when my boss said "Galilea," the word at first meant nothing to me, perhaps because the annoying way he pronounced the word robbed it of its power. And biblical names were usually relegated to our poorest neighbor-hoods—Belencito, Siloé, Nazaret—so I didn't give it a sec-ond thought.

Twenty minutes later I was in a taxi, heading for Galilea. The driver had never even heard of the place and had to radio for directions.

All I knew about angels was a prayer I used to recite as a child:

> *Sweet Guardian Angel*
> *My heavenly guide*
> *Hovering, night and day*
> *Gently by my side.*

My only contact with angels had been in grade school, at a procession on the thirteenth of May in honor of the Virgin Mary, and it had not turned out well. It so happened that one year, for being such a model student, my best friend, Marie Chris Cortés, had been chosen to be part of the Ce-lestial Legion and had to wear an angel costume with a pair of very real-looking wings, which her mother had made for her out of real feathers. When I saw her, I laughed, and told her she looked more like a chicken than an angel, which was true. It was traditional on that day for each girl to write down on a piece of paper her secret wish to the Immaculate Virgin Mary, which nobody else could read or else it wouldn't come true. These papers were put in an earthen jar and burned so that the smoke would reach up to Heaven. On this occasion, Marie Chris Cortés, offended by my comment about the chicken, snatched the piece of paper from my hands and read it out loud. And so it was that the whole school found out that I had asked to please one day be able to see our mother superior's shaved head. For some reason, this provoked a sublime indignation in the aforementioned person, which, in my opinion, was totally out of proportion with the offense. As punishment, I was summoned to her private quarters, terrifying enough in itself, and when we were alone, she took off her wimple and showed me her head, which was not shaved but had closely cropped gray hair. She made me touch it and then apologize. I still remember that moment as one of the scariest of my life, although now I think it really wasn't such a big deal. Quite the contrary, for a time it was a real distinction: I was the only girl in the school who had not only seen, but actually touched, the shorn head of a nun—and not just any nun, but the mother superior. To preserve the myth, I swore it was as bald as a billiard ball, and I have never revealed the truth until now.

But getting back to *Somos* and the article I had to write: the motives for selecting the angel story seemed despicable. In spite of that, my mood had improved. After all, even this was preferable to having to ask Miss Antioquia her views on extramarital relationships.

Submerged in the slow polluted sea of buses, cars, and beggars in the irregular streets of this chaotic city, we took an hour and a half to drive from north to south. Then we arrived at the poor neighborhoods on the mountainside and continued until the streets disappeared. It had started raining, and the taxi driver announced:

"This is as far as I can go. You'll have to walk from here."

"All right."

"Are you sure you want me to leave you here? You'll get wet."

"Which way do I go?"

He answered with a vague gesture toward the invisible mountain peak.

"Up."

No wonder there are angels there, I thought. It's practically in heaven.

For a long stretch I walked uphill in the rain. This Galilea was a frightful place. Above it, the rugged mountain rose like a wall; on either side grew a tangled mass of woodland vegetation; below, a dense, spongy haze filled the ravine so completely that it was impossible to see all the way down.

The houses in Galilea were precariously perched one on top of the other, clawing into the eroded, slippery hillside. Rainwater rushed down the steep alleys, forming little streams. The heart of the neighborhood was a swampy square with an arch on either side indicating that, in better weather, it was a soccer field. If a ball got away, it would roll on and on, and not stop until it reached Bolívar Square.

There was nobody on the streets, not even thieves. Not a voice could be heard behind the closed doors. The one ubiquitous presence was the rain, a nasty freezing rain that fell on me with the impersonal and relentless rhythm of a machine. Where were the people? They had probably left for less vile places. And what about the angel? Better forget it. If he had come down to earth and landed here, he must have fled back at once.

I felt an urgent need to go to the bathroom, to return home, take a hot shower, have a cup of tea, call my magazine and resign. I had reached a state of total desperation.

But how to get back, by which unimaginable taxi or bus, considering that I had crossed the frontier of the world and was now high above at the border of the great beyond?

I walked to the church, recently and meticulously painted banana yellow, its doors and trim in gleaming brown. Oversized and flashy, and with a pair of spiky steeples, it looked like a freshly baked Gothic cake. It was also closed, so I rang the bell at the rectory next door. No answer. I rang again, longer, banged at the door with my fist, until an old man's voice yelled from the other side of the door:

"There's nothing! Nothing!"

I had been taken for a beggar. I banged again, more insistently, and again heard the voice inside.

"Go away, there's nothing!"

"All I want is information!"

"There isn't any information either."

"How can that be? Come on!" I was now indignant and ready to kick the door, but it finally opened, and the voice acquired the body of a priest, old but not ancient, with glasses, nicotine-stained teeth, several days' stubble, and a soup bowl in his hand. His head was not round but shaped in straight lines, like a polygon, and I imagined it could produce only obtuse ideas.

From inside the house came the stench of an inveterate smoker's den.

"Father, I am here because I was told about an angel," I said, trying to press myself under the eaves for some relief from the rain.

Annoyed, he mumbled that he didn't know anything about an angel. Pieces of carrots were floating in his soup and, through his glasses, his impatient eyes told me that his lunch was getting cold. But I persisted.

"I was told that an angel—"

"No! No! What's this about angels? I'm telling you there is no angel!" the old man reprimanded me, and ended by saying that if I really wanted to praise the Lord and listen to his true word, I should come back and attend the five o'clock mass.

I figured the old guy was a bit loony, but since I desperately had to use the toilet, I had no choice.

"Excuse me, Father, could I use your bathroom?"

He considered the question for a moment, perhaps trying to figure out an excuse to say no, but then stepped aside to let me in. "Through the corridor in the yard, all the way to the back," he grumbled.

His home was an almost empty room with a door to the street and another to the yard. It seemed as if no one else had visited for years. Only some plastic flowers in a jar, barely visible under a coat of dust, suggested a possible feminine presence long ago.

"You are soaked, my child, take your coat off."

"Don't worry, Father, it's all right."

"No, it's not all right. You're dripping on my floor."

I apologized and tried to wipe the puddle dry with a tissue I found in my pocket. I took off my raincoat and hung it on the wall, on the nail that he had indicated.

I crossed to an inner yard where several drains converged, and as I walked along the corridor lined with plantless planters, containing only dried-up soil and cigarette butts, I thought that the priest's bristly beard must be quite rough, like porcupine quills. For a moment I tried to imagine how I would fend him off if he tried to touch me.

Though no stranger had ever assaulted me, at times I had somewhat paranoid thoughts of how I would prevent an attack. This time my irrationality annoyed me: How could I think such nonsense, when it was obvious that the poor old man only wanted to be left to eat his soup in peace?

Except for a small pile of half-washed socks in the bathtub, the bathroom was pretty clean. But I did not sit on the toilet; since early childhood I had been trained in the acrobatics of peeing standing up when not at home, without touching the toilet or wetting my pants. The door had no lock, so I held it shut with my arm extended, in case someone (but, my God, who?) were to try to open it. That's why I feel that a woman's psyche is at times twisted: we have been made to believe that all the bad things in the world are threatening us, trying to get between our legs.

There was no mirror in the bathroom. I missed it, because I find it reassuring to inspect my image. There was a shelf with only one object on it: a toothbrush with yellow bristles stained from overuse, which involuntarily connected me to the intimate loneliness of the surly man who lived there.

When I got back to the room, he was sitting on the cot, devoted to his soup, his face so close to the bowl that the steam was fogging his glasses.

"So there is no angel." This was my last attempt.

"The angel, the angel, there we go again with the angel! Doesn't it occur to anyone that he might be an envoy from the underworld, huh? And what if the unmentionable is using some cunning to drag the ignorant masses to their damnation? Hasn't this occurred to you?"

"So you think this angel might be a demon?"

"I already told you. Come to the five o'clock mass! Today is the day. I will publicly unmask the heretics in this neighborhood, who are of the same stripe as the old ones: Dionysius the pseudo Areopagite, Adalbert the Hermit"—his priestly zeal was making him shake. "They are even greater sinners, these ones from Galilea, than Simon the Magician, who falsely asserted that the world was made out of the same stuff as the angels. Let today's apostates tremble before anathema! They better not play with fire, huh? Because they'll get burned! But don't make me go on. Enough! I don't want to say anything ahead of time!" Here he paused to catch his breath and wipe his mouth with a handkerchief. "Come to the five o'clock mass if you want to understand."

"All right, I'll be there, Father. Good-bye, and thank you for letting me use your bathroom."

"Oh, no. Now that you are here, you can't leave without

having some soup. Because it is true that he who eats alone dies alone, and I don't want to die alone. It's bad enough to have lived all my life without companionship."

"No, Father, don't trouble yourself." I tried to dissuade him, neither wishing to deprive him of his only pleasure nor wanting to have to taste those shipwrecked carrots in the gray broth. But to no avail: he walked up to the pot and filled a bowl to the brim, then pulled a squashed packet of Lucky Strikes from his cassock and lit one at the stove.

"How come you live so alone, Father? Don't your parishioners keep you company?"

"They don't like me. Perhaps because when I came to these hills I was already old and bitter and didn't feel any great impulse to make them love me. But don't make me talk after lunch; it is bad for digestion and does not contribute to an orderly train of thought."

In silence, then, I ate and he smoked, if silence is the word for the sequence of noises and crackling sounds the old man let loose while savoring the stinking smoke of his cigarette. The soup tasted better than it looked, my stomach welcomed the hot liquid, and I appreciated my host's rough generosity. He had meanwhile fallen asleep sitting on his cot, the lit butt between his yellow fingers and his polygon head hanging at an impossible angle.

I took the cigarette from his hand, stubbed it out in one of the planters, washed his dish and mine in the bathroom washstand, left a note that read "God bless you, at five I'll be at your mass," and again walked out into the raging wind and rain. But I didn't mind anymore, now that I was sure I would have a story to tell. My curiosity was piqued: I really wanted to find out what kind of creature this angel of Galilea was. Besides, at the five o'clock mass there could be excommunications, or even threats of death by burning at the stake. I wouldn't miss that for the world.

I wandered around until I came to a store named La Estrella, where I ordered a café au lait and a semisweet roll with guava jelly.

In La Estrella all items essential for the survival of the neighborhood were squeezed into a space under three hundred square feet. There were lightbulbs, yards of fabric, lard, plastic toys, rice, sausage, nail polish, razor blades, aspirin, thongs, and chinaware—everything prodigiously organized and displayed on wooden shelves that reached all the way to the ceiling. There were also some long tables with benches, where lunch and beer were served, as indicated on a penciled sign.

"Do you know anything about the angel that has appeared around here?"

I was asking the elderly couple behind the counter. They looked at each other. They were probably husband and wife but looked enough alike to be brother and sister. Maybe they were. With ceremonial hand gestures, like bishops dispensing their blessings, they were fanning away flies.

"Pardon my impertinence," the old man said, bowing his head as if he were really asking to be forgiven. "Did you just ask Father Benito that same question?"

I noticed that from La Estrella you could see the rectory

door. They had been spying on me, of course, but that was understandable. Surely not too many strangers came up to Galilea.

"Is the parish priest's name Benito?" I inquired.

"The parish priest's name is Father Benito," they corrected me gently.

"Well, yes, sir. I did ask him."

"And what did Father Benito tell you, if you don't mind my asking?" The old man sounded pretentious.

"That there wasn't any."

They again exchanged knowing glances, and the old lady said: "Don't pay any attention to him. He's a reactionary priest."

I thought this old lady with her Maoist jargon must know a lot. I was about to question her when she beat me to it.

"Are you a reporter, miss?"

"Yes, ma'am."

"I can tell because of your camera. May I ask for what kind of publication?"

"For *Somos* magazine."

"Congratulations," the old man said. "It's a very well-known magazine. I presume, young lady, you have your ID?"

"My press ID?" The question surprised me. "Yes, I do."

"May I see it for a moment, if it's not too much trouble?"

This was unreal. In this militarized country, corporals, lieutenants, and patrol-car officers are constantly asking you for your documents, but up until now I had never had to identify myself to a shopkeeper. Still, I figured nothing bad could come of it with someone who bowed his head that courteously, so I pulled my press ID from my wallet and handed it to him. This was, of course, an irrational move, the first of many.

The two old inquisitors disappeared behind the counter and I heard them whispering. Then the man walked to the door and, with shouts and whistles, called "Orlando." After a short while, a boy appeared. He was about ten years old, perhaps older, judging from his worldly-wise look; or perhaps younger, considering how skinny and runty he was. The eyes of this boy were like a young calf's, all black irises with full, long eyelashes, and he was missing a tooth—it was anybody's guess whether it had not grown in yet or whether he had already lost it.

The old man handed him my ID, the old woman gave him a large piece of cardboard so that he could protect himself from the rain, and Orlando left. I watched him disappear with my only ID, and saw how he skipped around the corner, taking short, tight steps in that style of walking in the rain so typical of the people of Bogotá and so impossible for others to imitate. The old man must have noticed my distressed look, because he poured me another cup of coffee and said, "Don't worry, he is a very responsible boy."

I did not understand what was happening, but it was reassuring to know that Orlando was a responsible boy. While I waited for him to return, a woman in rubber boots came into the store and asked for two aspirins, four steel nails, and a dozen matches. The elderly couple opened the corresponding jars, counted out the required quantities, wrapped each of them in brown paper, and placed the jars back on the shelves. The woman paid with a few coins and left.

Orlando made good his reputation of being a responsible boy and was back fifteen minutes later with my ID, which he returned to me. Then he stood at the center of the store and, sounding like a town crier, announced: "Señora Crucifija says everything is in order, *La Monita* may go up."

La Monita, Blondie, that was me. It's always the same, poor people invariably call me that. What's more, they never care to ask me my first name, much less my family name. For them, it has always been Monita. My hair is to blame, this mass of blond hair that I have always kept long. It does not attract much attention among the wealthy but to the poor it seems sensational. My hair is considered exotic in this corner of the world. That and my height, which is six inches above average, are a legacy from my Belgian grandfather. At work, I wear my hair in a single tight plait, which is more comfortable and less showy than wearing it loose. That's how I was wearing it that first day I went up to Galilea. But it did not matter, it never does. The boy called me Monita and I would be known as Monita to the end.

Orlando had brought along an assorted bunch of kids, all dripping wet.

"Go ahead, they'll take you there," the old man said, pointing at them. "Right, dear?"

"That's right," the old lady agreed. "Don't worry, they'll take you."

"Oh, all right," I said, without asking where; I had learned that this matter had its own bureaucracy and its own mystery. When I noticed that the boys all wore Croydon rubber boots, I realized this must be the fashion around the Galilea mud holes and asked the couple if they would sell me a pair.

"What size do you wear, young lady?"

"Size nine," I answered, knowing that they would not carry that size. Their largest pair was actually a seven, so I resigned myself to the sneakers I had on. I put on my raincoat, thanked the old lady for the piece of cardboard she offered me as an umbrella, and left, following my Sherpa guides.

It was raining much harder now, the wind was blowing hysterically, and the ground was pure mud. I thought that if it continued raining like this, Galilea would slide all the way down to Bolívar Square, and before actually sinking my shoes into the muddy waters, I invoked another image with some nostalgia: Oh, to be with a roof over my head right now, Miss Cauca, and asking you whether the cucumber face mask is the ideal one for your complexion!

As I was trotting along in the rainstorm with my entourage of kids soaked to the skin, I tried to get Orlando to tell me where they were taking me. He raised his eyebrows and shrugged his shoulders, as if it were obvious:

"Well, to see the angel, of course!"

"Does he appear at about this time?"

"He is always there."

"Oh, so it's a statue, or a painting?"

He looked at me in amazement, unable to fathom such stupidity.

"It's no painting, it's an *a-n-g-e-l*," he said, spelling it out as if I had trouble with the language. "A real flesh-and-blood angel."

I was not expecting this. I had imagined that, with some luck, I would be able to interview a witness to one of his miracles, or a cult follower, or, in the best of circumstances, some sick person he had healed, and then maybe I could photograph the rock on which he had stood, the niche where candles are lighted in his honor, the cliff where he first appeared—all the routine junk that would satisfy the requirements of my editor, that would allow him to patch together in a couple of hours a story that made little sense but would justify a headline on the cover like "Angels in Colombia too!" followed by, "True accounts of sightings."

But Orlando was promising me the real angel, an opportunity to see him in the flesh.

"And where does the angel live?" I pressed him.

"With his mother."

"He has a mother?"

"Like everybody else."

"Ah, yes, of course. And is his mother that Señora Crucifija who authorized me to come up?"

"No, his mother is Señora Ara."

I thought that I risked exasperating my guide with my next question, but I asked anyway.

"Can you tell me which angel we are talking about?"

"That's the problem, we still don't know."

"How's that?"

"We don't know. He has not wanted to reveal his name," Orlando said, and one of the other boys confirmed, "It's true, he hasn't."

We walked as far as the foot of the last street. Then it ascended, long and vertical, squeezed between two rows of low houses, each supporting the next like playing cards. There were no people around, only water skipping down. In that way it was a street just like the others, except it was more picturesque. The woodland greenery, with its exuberant fronds and mosses, crept over the tile roofs, which were decorated with a gaudily colorful zigzag of plastic garlands, surely nonbiodegradable remnants from the past feast of some patron saint.

Orlando pointed upward.

"That is Barrio Bajo. The angel lives up there, in the pink house."

"Which is Barrio Bajo?"

"This street."

"Why is it called Bajo, when it's actually higher than the others?"

"Because the poorest people live here."

"Well, let's go up."

I bent over to roll up my jeans, covered almost to my knees in the chocolate-brown water carrying all the garbage down with it.

"No, wait here under the eaves," a little girl in a red coat who was part of the entourage told me, and as if by magic, she disappeared, together with the rest of the kids, including Orlando. I waited where I was told, pressing my back to the wall to evade the water cascading from the roof. Time began to drag.

"Orlando! Orlaaandoo!" My hopeless shouts were no sooner born than extinguished, like candles in the wind.

In that alley the minutes dragged by, and I continued waiting, in my quiet corner, with the growing fear that the kids had taken cover in their homes, were drinking cups of hot milk, and had completely forgotten about me. This situation was already getting me down, when I saw them return in twos and threes, carrying boards.

Orlando seemed to be in charge of the operation: following his instructions, the children fluttered around, placing the boards across the narrow, unpaved alley, with each end balanced on stones on opposite sides, thus fashioning a sort of stairway of five or six steps, under which the water flowed. The girl in the red coat took my hand and led me up, step by step. As soon as my feet left a board, the others immediately removed it and put it down again ahead of me, so that the stairway preceded me up the hill, by a few steps.

I felt as blessed as Jacob ascending to heaven on the angels' ladder. These smiling creatures, so eager for me to proceed comfortably in the midst of the downpour, prompted a sudden premonition, which would return very clearly at times while I was in Galilea: I was entering a realm not of this earth.

"You are not the first reporter to come here," Orlando explained.

"Have there been many?"

"Quite a few. One came with television cameras. People

from other neighborhoods too. From Loma Linda, from La Esmeralda . . . They have even come from Fontibón to see—"

"Your angel must be very important."

"Very true, he is magnificent."

I thought the word *magnificent* sounded funny coming from a boy, and I asked him if he had also seen the angel.

"Of course, we have all seen him because he lets himself be seen."

"Have you spoken with him?"

"No, I haven't. He speaks with no one."

"Why doesn't he?"

"He does talk, see, but mostly to himself. We don't understand what he says."

"Why not?"

"Because we don't understand his languages."

"So how many does he speak?"

"I would say about twenty or twenty-five. I don't know."

"It seems that the priest does not believe in the angel."

"He does believe, but he denies it. See, he is jealous of him."

"Jealous of the angel? But why?"

"Because he has become a very popular angel. And besides, the priest is afraid of him. That must be it, he is afraid of him."

"Afraid? How?"

"Well, sometimes he is a terrible angel."

This last phrase hit me. But I could ask no further questions; we had arrived at the pink house, and the kids were milling around, making a lot of noise. It was a hovel, one of those partially built shacks that are never quite finished but "improved" with planks and pieces of cardboard, pots with flowers, bleeder cables for pirated electricity, radios at full blast, and powerful television antennae.

Orlando knocked on the door, and I was overcome with a strange uneasiness. What kind of a creature was I about to behold? Possibly some freak of nature. I took a deep breath and braced myself for the worst.

The house was dark inside and the air heavy with smoke and incense. Six or seven women praying on their knees nailed me with their eyes as if using voodoo pins on a rag doll. Then, feigning indifference, they returned to their prayers, though every now and then I felt the stab of their inquisitive stares.

Orlando, the only kid who came in with me, pulled at my jeans for me to kneel, which I did. Then he pointed to the leader, a woman armed with a rosary. Distressingly skinny and dressed all in black, she had a bloodcurdling face, which lacked something essential. I watched her out of the corner of my eye to inspect her every feature: her eyes were in the right place, and also her nose, mouth, and chin. The thing her face lacked was expression, which made her appear ghoulish.

"That's Sister María Crucifija, president of the council," Orlando whispered.

"Of what council?"

"Of the council that takes care of the angel."

"And the angel's mother?"

"She isn't here right now."

"And the one with the blue cape?" I asked about a tiny woman wrapped in an improbable royal blue velvet cape. "Does she also belong to the council?"

"Yes, her name is Marujita de Peláez."

"The cape she's wearing, is it for ceremonies?"

"No, it's for when it rains."

"That gigantic woman," I said and pointed discreetly to a bulky woman who was praying with a devotion and meekness out of keeping with her size. "Who is she?"

"That's Sweet Baby Killer, a former wrestling champion, very famous here in Galilea. Another council member. She used to be very tough, especially when we yelled '*Hombra*' at her, which was her nickname. But ever since she joined the council, she has calmed down. You can even call her Hombra, and she won't turn on you. And the thing is, you know, not everyone in Colombia can pronounce Sweet Baby Killer right."

Orlando evidently could. What's more, he said it with a gum-chewing drawl, like Tom Hanks in *Forrest Gump*.

"I understand. Are there any men in the council?"

"Not a one. Only women."

"Then the nun is the one in charge?"

"What nun?"

"Well, Sister María Crucifija, of course."

"She is no nun. She is a laywoman. She'll tell you when it's time for you to go up and see him."

"The angel? Where is he?"

"He hides in what we call the Bethel Grottoes, up the mountain."

More people were arriving, half a dozen men and women who meekly settled in the corners without bothering anyone, without taking up much space. They were pilgrims, Orlando told me, and some were carrying offerings. I noticed that the inside of the house did not look like the usual impoverished hovel, where eight kids, three beds, two rocking chairs, a dining table with six chairs and a cupboard, an icebox, stools, small tables, dogs and chickens, colanders, pots, and crockery are harmoniously organized in less than fifty square feet of space. This house was different—more spacious, emptier, and the objects in it, as well as the people, seemed suspended in air.

Time was passing; I kept expecting something to happen, but nothing did; only one Hail Mary after another. Sister María Crucifija would call them out in a high trill, and the rest of us would chant in lower tones, and thus the praying seemed to go on forever, like the limitless dark blue sea. My knees could not take any more penance.

"Orlando," I asked, "couldn't I talk with Sister Crucifija for a minute?"

"You can't interrupt. It's forbidden."

"I don't want to pray anymore."

"We still have to wait until it stops raining."

Another four mysteries of the rosary went by before the rain finally ceased, and certain movements in the house indicated that the important moment had come. Sister María Crucifija disappeared, then returned and started dispatching orders.

"The women with mantillas, the men bareheaded!"

Her little face looked like it had been incinerated. She approached each of us, taking us by the arm and positioning us, single file, close to the door. At times she was not satisfied with someone's placement and moved them ahead or back—God knows for what reason, since it was not a matter of height—and she led us out to the street in this formation, like Snow White's seven dwarfs. I looked toward the mountain and had the feeling I was on my way to an unpleasant encounter.

"You also came to meet the angel?" I asked the man with a hat who was standing behind me.

"I already have. I came to bring him this offering of gratitude; he saved my granddaughter from certain death," he answered, and showed me a hen, its legs tied, that looked even more confused than I was.

I did not want to lose Orlando's comforting company, but María Crucifija announced that the boy could not go up, as minors were not admitted on Mondays and Thursdays. I asked why, but the woman was there to give orders, not explanations.

Other logistical barriers had to be overcome, such as my not having something to cover my head. My neighbor was wearing a hat, so I asked him to lend it to me. But I was not yet acceptable.

"You can't go in wearing pants," Crucifija told me. My raincoat was a long, belted trenchcoat with buttons all the way down, so I closed it tightly and took my jeans off right then and there.

"Now I am not wearing pants anymore," I said.

"But you can't take the camera."

"I have to take at least one photo."

"You can't. The flash frightens him."

I explained, I begged, but to no avail. I had to surrender my camera to Marujita de Peláez, the lady in the blue cape. To me this spelled disaster. It was getting late and I still had no story; I had seen nothing that would be of interest to *Somos*. And now there wouldn't be any photos, so no matter what kind of story I wrote my boss was going to kill it.

At last we started moving, but we had not taken more than twenty steps before a new problem arose. This was the most outrageous of them all.

Stopping the flow of the line, Sister Crucifija again clawed my arm, pulled me aside, and asked:

"Can you tell me if you are with the visit?"

"The visit? What visit?"

"I mean, if you are having your period . . ."

I imagined we were dealing with some atavistic belief, such as that in the mere presence of menstrual blood, wine would turn sour or iron would rust, and God knows what could happen to angels. I was afraid that such matters might prevent me from entering the grotto.

"No, sister. I'm clean," I answered truthfully, also thinking it was the best answer under the circumstances.

"Can you tell me exactly when your last menstruation started?"

That was too much. The so-called Crucifija behaved not only like a misogynistic biblical character but like a gynecologist during a six-month checkup. I was at the point of consigning her and her angel to the bottomless pit and, while I was at it, throwing *Somos* in too. But I controlled myself. What could I lose by answering? It was impossible for me to remember the exact date—I have never kept records of my periods—so I answered whatever came to mind:

"Exactly fifteen days ago."

I assume I gave the right answer, because she let me get back in line with the others, and we started to climb the mountain along a muddy path fringed by wet broom plants and acacia mimosas.

"Those seeds are very poisonous, don't eat them," my neighbor warned me, pointing to the many green pods along the way.

At no point had I ever thought of eating them, but I thanked him for his advice anyway.

We did not have to go far. In less than ten minutes we reached a cleft in the rock, half-covered by a boulder. We were at the mouth of the grottoes.

The excitement I had felt a couple of hours earlier had dissipated; by now I was exhausted and felt reluctant to enter the grotto. The angel had disappointed me already, so sure was I that this was a hoax set up by some wise guy or, worse, a hoax set up by honest folks. As we waited, my distaste for the whole spectacle kept growing. Who might be locked up in there? A hermaphrodite? A leper? The Elephant Man or Kasper Hauser? Who was this poor victim of superstition and ignorance?

Sister María Crucifija issued some more warnings, this time for the whole group.

"You are about to enter the Bethel Grottoes, the abode of the angel. You have to take off your shoes and leave them at the entrance, because you are about to step on Holy Ground. Once inside, you are to sing the hymn to the Holy Trinity, the seraphic hymn, the only language an angel understands. Don't say anything else, because all other human sounds bother him. In case you don't know it, the hymn to the Holy Trinity goes like this: "Holy, holy, holy. Holy is the Lord.""

"Holy, holy, holy. Holy is the Lord . . .""

"Those of you bringing animals should leave them here. Also any offerings or gifts. You should not give food to the angel, nor frighten him with screams, nor try to touch him. Do not lag behind, because you'll get lost. Everybody must leave the grottoes at the same time."

Crucifija rattled off her instructions like a flight attendant reciting the list of safety measures. I closed my eyes so I would not see my neighbor twisting the hen's neck before leaving it there as an offering, but he didn't; he placed it where he was told, next to a plastic bag with some figs.

With a shove of her powerful shoulder, Sweet Baby Killer

moved the boulder that blocked the entrance. When my turn came, I bent down to go through the opening and was struck by a disturbing, humid odor. It smelled like the center of the earth, I thought, and perhaps also, by association, like the scent of eternity. Or of the grave? Yes, perhaps it smelled more like a grave.

The space inside was becoming darker and wider, so with each step we could straighten up a bit. We were following Sister Crucifija, who held a torch with weak batteries. "Holy, holy, holy"—we entered the darkness holding on to one another because we could hardly see anything—"Holy is the Lord," and the soles of our feet resented the icy loam on the slippery floor of the cave.

We measured each step as if a chasm might lie just ahead. The ceiling of the cave arched upward until we could no longer touch it with our hands. I felt a breeze on my face and thought I had reached a large empty chamber. The whole thing was preposterous—"Holy, holy, holy"—with me standing barefoot in the belly of the planet, wearing a trenchcoat and someone else's hat, repeating the word *holy,* and not knowing whether I was shivering from cold, excitement, or fear.

"We have to wait here," Crucifija ordered, as her flashlight's anemic beam danced erratically about, revealing patches of the cave wall.

It's not much fun waiting in the dark for a stranger to appear, even less if you assume he has wings and can come swooping down on you. Our group was getting nervous and drew closer together, while the chanting of the hymn to the

Holy Trinity, our only means of connecting to the supernatural, grew louder. I was having my doubts about the breeze I felt: Was it really the wind, or perhaps bats zooming down too close? Were there rats running around on the ground? It was impossible to figure out how much time had passed, we had abandoned the temporal world outside. Claustrophobia—or was it anxiety?—was tightening my throat.

Every now and then someone coughed, and the echo answered, "Holy, holy, holy. Holy is the Lord . . ."

I heard sounds like the crackling of a fire or the rush of underground streams. Or perhaps it was just the darkness murmuring. Suddenly my neighbor whispered:

"I can tell he's near . . ."

"The angel?" My voice was a sigh.

"Yes."

"How do you know?"

"Can't you feel it? Don't you sense his presence in the air?"

All I could feel was a greater tightening in my throat, and then I saw Crucifija beam her flashlight onto the small mirror of her compact in order to project what seemed like fast, intermittent light signals. In any case, I answered yes, that I sensed it, and perhaps I was not lying. Then I saw *him.*

Without a sound to announce his presence and seemingly out of nowhere, a youth appeared. Very tall. Almost naked. Raven-haired. Overwhelmingly handsome. That was all. And it was too much. My heart thumped in my breast and then stopped; my soul failed me when I saw him. He was only a youth, and yet, I was certain he was something else as well, a creature from another level of reality.

He had the calm, undulating movements of sea creatures, or of mimes, and his bearing was at the same time humble and majestic, like that of a deer. He remained before us for only a few seconds, without making a sound, without making contact, but without recoiling either, as if unaware of us. We could not keep our eyes off him; he, in contrast, looked through us, looked without seeing, and I understood why: veiled by the darkness of the grotto, we were blotted out, mere black smudges against a black background, while he burned like a contained fire, radiant with an incandescent light that seemed to emanate from his skin.

At the exit of the grottoes, Orlando was waiting for me with the news that Doña Ara, the angel's mother, wanted to show me her journals.

"What journals?"

"You'll see."

Orlando and I started to walk down toward the pink house, although I would have much preferred to be alone for a moment to clear my mind. The Angel of Galilea had disturbed me.

He was the most disquieting creature I had ever seen. Everything about that youth defied reason: the mystery surrounding him, his overwhelming serenity, his luminous presence. And his beauty . . . an absolutely irresistible beauty, a supernatural beauty.

On the other hand, everything else about his story was outrageous. What was this creature doing locked up in the dark, inside a cave, naked in the biting cold, subject to the whims of a madwoman like Crucifija? My first impulse was to find a telephone and seek help, I don't know from whom, perhaps a doctor, someone from human rights, or the police. No, not the police, they would organize a rescue operation that would result in the angel's death.

Or was the young man himself an accessory to the hoax? A willing participant in the spectacle? I was unable to fathom what he could gain from it. It did not seem to be money; at least so far I had not seen anybody charging for anything, except the voluntary offerings, and no one would agree to such a charade in exchange for an old hen and a bag of figs. Perhaps the young man himself was honestly convinced that he was an angel.

Or perhaps he really was . . . Why not? After seeing him, it was easier to entertain such a possibility.

As I listened to the mutterings of the other grotto visitors, I was surprised to learn why they did not share my excitement.

"It seems to me you did not come out of the grottoes very convinced," I said to my neighbor who had lent me his hat.

"The angel failed us this time," he said with resignation.

"But why? He did show up, and he was splendid."

"Yes, but he didn't *do* anything."

I thought I understood his comment. For a man to get enthusiastic, things have to happen, while for a woman, things just have to be.

Orlando was pulling me by the hand, and I let him lead me. When we arrived at the pink house, he brought me to a small room where a woman was feeding a coal stove, letting the flames light up her beautiful face. I noticed that she was almost my age, and I could glimpse in her features those of the angel. She was his mother, no doubt about it: I'd never seen such a resemblance between two people.

Lying open on the table, there was a graph-paper notebook, line after line filled with compact handwriting, each word ending fancifully in an upward flourish like a little mouse tail.

"He dictates and I write everything down," Ara told me, gently turning the pages of the journal. "This is book number fifty-three. The other fifty-two are over there." She pointed to a tin trunk locked with a padlock.

"See, Monita, there are fifty-two journals, fifty-three with this one," Orlando added, but Doña Ara kept on talking without hearing him.

"I have been writing for nine years. My son started to dictate to me before he returned."

She explained all without my having to ask her. Her newborn baby had disappeared, and seventeen years later, just two years ago, she had gotten him back. I did not ask her a thing; she kept on talking with the painful compulsion of someone who has had to repeat the story a thousand times, like a dog licking a wound that never heals.

"My son's father was only a shadow, without a face or a name," she said. "He came out of the wilderness one night, threw me on the ground, and afterward turned into a column of smoke. I managed to notice that he wore a ring on his right hand and that his clothes had the smell of camphor.

"He did not have me long, barely enough to get me pregnant. I had just turned thirteen, and my father had arranged for me to marry a wealthy man, an older man who owned a truck. That's why my father didn't like the news at all.

"He did not want me to bear the child and took me to a woman who gave me a bitter potion to drink and pricked my insides with knitting needles. I threw up and then was bleeding, but the baby had decided to stay and grew bigger and bigger, paying no attention to my father's fury or his evil threats.

"The baby was getting so big it started to be noticeable that I was pregnant. My father with his fits of rage had turned into a vicious tiger. Until one day, without a word, he took me to the countryside and kept me hidden so that the man he wanted me to marry wouldn't see me. God knows what he told him, that I was sick, perhaps, or that he would not bring me to him until the day of our wedding.

"When my baby was born, I did not see him much. Just as I had not seen the father, I hardly saw the son. He was quickly taken away from me, but I did notice he was exceedingly beautiful, and his skin had a luminous glow. His eyes were wide open from the very beginning, and I also saw that his gaze was so deep that he could see the depths of one's soul.

"I wanted to know if he smelled of camphor, because I thought he would inherit that from his father. But he only smelled like me, like my own blood, my own scent.

"He was taken away from me almost immediately, but not before I was able to put a gold medal of the Virgin of the Winds around his neck, the one I had worn all my life.

After that, I never saw my baby again. I asked for him every day, until my mother finally had mercy on me and confessed the truth.

"That father of mine had sold him to some gypsies who passed through town with the circus, she said; that is how his life began, without a mother's love, traveling around the world and getting to know its hardships. I kept crying so hard, my mother tried to comfort me. 'Stop lamenting,' she said. 'If you don't, no one will want to marry you.'

"Then I cried even more, because I did not like the man I was supposed to marry, and all I wanted was my son. I dreamed of a kindly gypsy woman who would let him lick her finger after she had dipped it in sugar, and who would not let the circus beasts frighten him.

"The milk in my breasts dried up, and the time came when I was to be given to that man. But the damage was done, and the man, though old, would be able to notice that I had already lost my virginity. To marry a virgin, someone who had not known sin, had been his main condition. So my father then took me back to the same woman, who, in half an hour, performed the miracle of making me a virgin again, and so I became a virgin mother.

"She patched me up with spider webs and egg whites, and I left her house as if I were brand-new. They dressed me in white tulle, and I walked to the altar still with a poultice between my legs. But the old man was no fool, and as soon as he got me to bed, he discovered the deceit and returned me the same night.

"'Let her be an old maid then,' said that father of mine,

half-resigned to no longer being the father-in-law of a wealthy man. My mother confronted him, even daring to tell him, 'At least we could have kept the child, but you had to sell him, blinded by a gleaming truck.' In the belief that I no longer had a future, my parents took me to the parish priest and offered me for taking care of his personal housekeeping and that of the church. This priest was very old, and I had no complaints. He was good to me until the day he died; he taught me how to read the Scriptures and sing the Psalms. He used to let me out early, although he knew that my obsession was to go far from the neighborhood and roam about the city, in the streets and in the squares, searching for my son.

"I stood before every homeless street urchin, trying to recognize him. I did not let my untrustworthy eyes deceive me, because his looks could have changed, but trusted instead my more reliable nose. I sniffed each one of them as if I were a bloodhound, confident that I could recognize my own by his smell. I searched the orphanages, the circus tents, the open markets. Each day I went a little farther, until I got to where the city disintegrates into sheer misery. Each night I roamed, later and later into the night, and I checked the children who sell their bodies, and those who wake up in the morning on the sidewalk, covered with newspapers. I saw crippled children, burned children, others whose faces had become old before their time. I saw the child clowns, the shoe-shine kids, the street ragamuffins. I saw children pulling carts, selling pinwheels, hawking newspapers, singing country songs at movie theater exits. I smelled them all, and in none of them did I recognize my odor.

"Who could have believed that in a twist of fate I would finally encounter him, seventeen years after his birth, one day as I was standing right in front of my own home. Every single day I had looked for him, except that one, because I was worn out and depressed. And there I was when he slowly walked up to me, now grown up, with the shadow of a beard beginning to show on his boyish face, with those same eyes that peered deep into the soul from the first time he opened them. His beauty was not only intact, but rather enhanced so that it was impossible to look at him and not feel a weakness in your knees.

"He had an aura of sweetness and gentleness, like the waters of a vast placid lake. But he was silent. He did not speak then, just as he does not speak now. Words came out of his mouth, but they did not sound like a language; they sounded only like cooing, a murmuring of litanies, learned perhaps in other lands. That is why he could not tell me where he had been or what he had seen, how he had survived, or how he had found me.

"But he was my son, I could tell by his smell, and he also knew who I was, and that he was finally at my side, finally where he belonged.

"I did not regret that he could not speak; his silence was so deep and his presence so luminous that I realized no words were needed, and the pain of the long absence was better left unspoken. That's how things were, and that's how they had to be. And he rewarded me for my patience. In time he let me understand.

"It so happened that for seven years before his return, I

had fallen into a sort of trance every night, without fail, and sometimes also in the mornings, or even in the afternoons. The light would strike me, with no regard for the time of day or for what I was doing, or whether I was asleep or resting, and I had to grab my journal and start writing.

"The words I wrote down came from angels' voices; that's how Sister María Crucifija identified them the first time she read them. Not one angel, but many, a different one in every trance. In this way I started to accumulate journals, without really knowing who was dictating the words.

"The dictation did not cease with my son's return; on the contrary, it continued with such force that I started losing weight and became exhausted by such frenzied writing.

"The rest was simply a matter of putting two and two together. Sister María Crucifija revealed this to me, because she was the first one to understand it: The words that were not coming from my son's own lips were being revealed through my hand. The angel of my writings was my own son."

———

Yesterday, I was not, and tomorrow I shall no longer be. It is only during this infinite moment that I am the angel Orifiel, Throne of God, movable seat of the Father, and it is my everlasting joy to bear the weight of his powerful and vast buttocks. I am called Throne because God's majesty rests on me with utmost serenity and absolute peace. I am called Wheel, and I am called Chariot because I am the vehicle for Yahweh.

I am not matter, I tolerate no form, I am pure impact, explosion of energy, a blinding burst of light. I have no body but I have hundreds of feet: swift calves' hooves, bright as polished brass, spraying sparks as iron striking the anvil. I am fire and my flame is alive, I am a chariot and I devour space, I am a thunderbolt rumbling on the crests of time. I push stars from abyss to abyss, and I alone carry the Divine Horseman as He journeys through the celestial spheres. It is God himself who gallops on my shoulders, who sinks His spurs in my meek flanks and leaves a trail of incandescent spurts of my amber blood, obedient to His holy whims.

My head is one, but it has four faces; one looks north, another looks south, the third looks toward the dawn, and the fourth toward the setting sun, but each of them looks forward. I have four pairs of eyes but I see only God; four noses to perceive His essence; four pairs of ears to hear His echoes; four mouths that only praise His name, never despairing or needing rest, day in and day out until eternal exhaustion: Holy, holy, holy!

Holy is the Lord. His presence is so dynamic, and the ocean of His love is so engulfing that it stuns, destroys, annihilates, floods everything with its excessive burst of light. Much too much light! Everything else pales and disappears. Before my eyes, dazzled by Him, the world of men and women is barely mirrored behind curtains of liquid glass.

God is too big a word for me. Who am I, Orifiel, to dare say it? I am nothing dissolved in nothing, faithful dog, amazed servant prostrate on the ground on his four faces.

The Creator has allowed me access to all His glories, all His paradises, all His graces and radiance except one, which is fundamental: I am not wise enough to decipher Him. So far removed from my grasp is the mystery of His being, that an attempt at comprehension would hopelessly drag me into the sin of pride. I have more than enough by perceiving His reflections, by feeling His monumental weight on me, by hearing from His lips the orders I zealously obey before He can count to two: "Take burning embers, Orifiel, and cast them over that city," or else, "Your name will be Merkabah, Orifiel, and I shall ride in your chariot!" or perhaps, "Bring me a piece of bread, Orifiel, I feel like being hungry!" (Whichever way His whim of great creator of worlds and inventor of names may take Him, today He calls me Orifiel, tomorrow Merkabah, yesterday Metatron, or any other of my seventy-two names.)

Unity I lack, as well as identity: I am not one, I am legion, I am and we are more than a thousand, a wheel within a wheel, within another wheel, and within that wheel yet another, up to the ten hosts that make up the concentric army of the Wheels and the Thrones. Let them not attempt to intercept us because we are unassailable. We burn with fever in the dizzying spiral of multiplicity, and columns of smoke emanate from our hands.

We are so infinite that we encompass galaxies and, at the same time, so infinitesimal that we fit on the head of a single pin. How overwhelming, how terrifying is the unimaginable number of angels who fit on the head of a pin!

We call ourselves Orifiel, Throne of God, repose of His intense endeavors. We call ourselves Orifiel, Wheel of God, vehicle of His everlasting voyages. We call ourselves Orifiel, and we are blessed among all angels because it is our privilege to suffocate from joy under God's pink buttocks.

The Angel
Without a Name

DOÑA ARA, THE YOUNG MADONNA OF SORROWS, WENT OUT AFTER promising that she would open the trunk for me that night. Her story moved me, so much that I was not sure which character was more fascinating, the angel or his mother.

I leafed quickly through the journal she had left with me, and took a few snapshots. I managed to read in full only that day's pages, dictated just a few hours earlier by a celestial being who called himself Orifiel, self-described as Throne or Wheel.

What I read totally baffled me. From where, really and truly, could these amazing journals possibly have come? They were far too simple to be an angel's pronouncements, and yet, how could anyone accept that they were written by the illiterate people of this poor neighborhood? Again and again I went over every line of the text, bewildered and mesmerized by an amazing creature who, in a fifty-page, graph-paper notebook, actually claimed to be the bearer of God Himself.

Who could have written this? Supposing that Ara was the author, I would have to admit one of three possibilities: she was inspired by another entity or source; her personality was more complex than it seemed; or she had simply copied the whole thing from somewhere else. Of course, hers was the most appealing hypothesis: that the angel's secret voice was her son's, which she perceived through some sort of telepathy and then transcribed. It was the most attractive and yet the least convincing theory, if you consider how far-fetched it would be for a boy who does not even speak the language to dictate these fragments, which I, as a reporter whose profession is writing, could not produce. But whether of human or divine origin, authentic or apocryphal, these journals were a revelation and a genuine mystery.

Orlando was looking at the pages over my shoulder.

"Look, he does know his name," I told him, pointing at a line from the most recent text. "It says here that this is the angel Orifiel speaking . . ."

"That's what he says today, but tomorrow he'll say something else."

I would have given a finger from my own hand to be able to continue reading, I was so greatly excited. I also felt cozy near the comforting warmth of the stove. Someone, in a gesture of welcome, had placed my blue jeans and sneakers by the fire to dry. But I had to stop reading and get out into the cold again because it was close to five in the afternoon, and I wanted to attend Father Benito's mass.

It was still pouring outside, and the mud was getting thicker. Although Orlando and I skidded rather than walked down to the church, we were late and arrived near the end of the sermon. The crowd inside, clad in woollen *ruanas,* was huddled together, and there was a wet-animal smell in the church. At the back, nailed to his cross, a huge Christ agonized, horribly beaten and bloody.

I could not see Father Benito but I could hear, only too loudly, his holy wrath, thunderous and distorted by the loudspeakers:

"That woman who dares tell us that she had a dream when pregnant . . . That woman who dreamed, she says, that she was giving birth to a calf and therefore knew her son would be blessed. Blasphemy! It reeks of blasphemy! And I ask you, isn't a calf just too much like a lamb? And who is the Lamb? It is no other than Jesus! I declare that here, in this parish, someone is trying to take the place of Jesus Christ!"

After his declaration about the calf, which I presumed was directed at Doña Ara, he quoted fragments of what the angel had dictated, one of which was authentic, I can attest, because it was the same one I had just read. The priest's intelligence operation against his enemies, the followers of the angel, was undoubtedly quick and efficient. Father Benito was particularly incensed by the mention of God's buttocks:

"He who blasphemes against the divine dignity could only be the filthy mouth of Satan himself!" The old loudspeakers vibrated, adding dramatic electronic effects to his words. "Only the libidinous beast would dare mention the immaculate intimate parts of the Most Chaste One!"

I decided to take pictures of Father Benito, who would play the bad guy in my article. (I could imagine how my boss would caption the photos: "Inquisition from the pulpit!") I walked up to the altar and started shooting, trying to catch the most eloquent of my subject's grimaces, of which there were many, especially since he spewed his words along with a cloud of smoke, a Lucky Strike stub hanging from his lower lip.

My mistake was in moving away from the crowd and setting foot on the steps of the altar, or in getting too close to it, or perhaps in not kneeling when I was supposed to, or somehow acting in a way that seemed disrespectful to the ceremony. Suddenly the parish priest began berating me with a cascade of maledictions, not mentioning me by name but looking at me fiercely, and shaking his finger at me, particularly when he referred to "the modern world" or "the perversions of the modern world." In one instance he said "the devil, the world, and the flesh," pointing three times at me with his index finger, once for each word.

I noticed a man who would not take his eyes off me. Though I did not know him, there was genuine rage in his face: I felt his sharp hatred aimed not only at me but also at the angel he considered an impostor, at foreigners, at challenging women, at everyone making fun of his God. Up to that point my adventure in Galilea had been quite surprising and basically uplifting. But the expression on that man's face made me realize that I was swimming in an undertow. This matter of the angel touched very sensitive chords. I observed the crowd around me and could feel its somber mood, tense with religious fanaticism.

Since I felt uncomfortable, and at the same time ashamed of having caused a disturbance, I withdrew to the penumbra of a lateral nave and slipped out before the mass was over. As I was leaving the church, I heard over the loudspeakers the priest's last roar: "Let the false angel reveal his true name, so that we know what we're dealing with!"

I invited Orlando to have dinner with me at La Estrella, which was friendly territory. I almost did not recognize the store, it looked so different at night, with its red lights and rancid air, sullen men drinking beer, bottles piled on the tables, and a trio of treble guitar, guitar, and maracas playing an infinitely sad ballad. Orlando and I were gobbling up some potato turnovers sprinkled with chili sauce when somebody announced: "The people from El Paraíso are coming!"

"It's the pilgrims from another neighborhood, El Paraíso, coming to visit the angel," Orlando explained, while he pocketed what remained of his turnover, emptied his soft drink in one gulp, and ran off.

"Do you sell men's pants?" I asked the unctuous shop owner, who, always conferring with his wife and bowing more often than a Japanese, showed me some drill pants in various sizes. I picked out a pair, together with a shirt, a flashlight and batteries, and some oranges. I paid for everything, and when I stepped out onto the street, Orlando had already disappeared into the crowd.

There were hundreds of people from El Paraíso. Men, women, and children waited in the rain, on foot, in crowded jeeps, on donkeys; there was even an invalid on a litter, as well as many sick and lame. A genuine court of miracles, clothed in unrelieved poverty and misshapen by a cruel Nature. It was not easy to join them, yet at the same time, I liked being a part of them: I have always thought life is most vibrant where it is toughest.

The newcomers congregated in the square in front of the church, while the people leaving mass crowded together on the atrium. The two enemy camps stood facing each other: on one side, the priest's followers; on the other, the angel's. It was a war of grim stares and competing hymns. The church crowd sang an overly sentimental prayer, which I knew from my school days:

> When sad and in tears,
> I call upon you.
> May you give me your hand,
> And your blessings too.

Meanwhile, those in the town square, in the rain, were belting out the seraphic hymn, "Holy, holy, holy, Holy is the Lord." I climbed the stairs to the atrium hoping I could spot Orlando from up there, and at some point, I unconsciously joined the better tune, "May you give me your hand," which lulled me back to the violet light filtering through the stained glass windows in my elementary school chapel. I was remembering with envy how Ana Carlina Gamo had become the nuns' pet for being the only girl in the choir who could sing the solo in Schubert's "Ave Maria," when I felt a tug on my coat.

"Let's go, Monita!"

It was Orlando, pulling me away from the atrium and returning me to the pilgrims. The rain had almost stopped, and torches were being lit. And in the early evening twilight, the procession started uphill with me and Orlando in the lead. The priest's followers stayed below and started to disperse. As poor as they were, they looked down upon the Barrio Bajo people and the other followers of the angel, despising them for being even poorer than themselves.

We were among the first to arrive at Doña Ara's house. The aroma of the newly washed eucalyptus trees permeated the air. I turned to look back and beheld a wondrous view: a deep darkness had spread over the sky, revealing below me a dazzling panorama.

It was as if I was looking down at the world from its highest point. Far below lay an immense ocean of twinkling points, a map of the incandescent city composed in lights: illuminated windows, streetlamps, car lights, burning stoves, the red and green eyes of traffic lights, cigarette embers, and neon signs duplicated in street puddles. The pilgrims from El Paraíso were zigzagging toward us, their torches forming a luminous snake, while above us, almost within reach, the Milky Way glowed softly. The universe seemed charged with signs, and I felt I might decipher them all.

The pilgrims had assembled at the holy place, waiting for the angel to appear. They had brought him their sick to be healed and their newly born to be baptized. The old came seeking consolation, the young for novelty, the sad ones in search of hope, the women love, the homeless shelter, the unfortunate a blessing.

It was not easy for me to comprehend how the appearance of an angel—such a far-fetched apparition, a certifiably crazy notion—had become so meaningful for this community. But it was evident that for these people the power of an angel was more real, more accessible, and more trustworthy than that of a judge, a policeman, or a senator, let alone a president of the Republic.

The gusts of wind from Barrio Bajo turned warm, carrying hot breath and hotter yearning, and heat from the lighted torches. The mass of pilgrims prayed and wept, their feet stuck in the mud and their hearts open to the sublime. Their fervor was such and their faith so contagious that, for a moment, even I, a nonbeliever, believed through them.

The stubborn angel was not making his appearance, and the crowd's expectations were increasing. Although my reasons were worldly, I, too, was anxiously waiting for him: Was he really as magnificent as he had seemed in the darkness of the cave? I wanted to know. Besides, for my article I needed its star, the Angel of Galilea, to do something, perform even a tiny little miracle, anything worth reporting.

The door of the house opened, and the crowd lunged forward. I was trapped in the human crunch and could hardly breathe. It was worse for Orlando, who was short; at least I could keep my nose above the others. People were pushing and crushing us and I feared that when the angel appeared, they would trample us in their attempt to touch him.

But it was not the angel who appeared: it was only Sister María Crucifija and the women of the council, who were now sprinkling holy water from a gourd onto the heads of the flock, reciting litanies, and begging for patience. They assured us we would get to see the angel, only later.

The practical needs of the people from El Paraíso began to be pressing, and the doors in Barrio Bajo opened to take care of them. Here a baby bottle was warmed up, there a bathroom was made available, somewhere else chairs were carried out for the ladies, someone from across the street brought ammonia for a pilgrim who had fainted.

With Orlando's help, I was taking photos and interviewing people, marveling at the amazing naturalness with which the poor face the ineffable.

I asked a lady on a stretcher, with bandaged legs, "Why did you come, madam?"

"I came for the angel to heal my sores. I can't walk because of them."

"Don't you think you would do better seeing a doctor?"

"A doctor? Last time I saw a doctor was in 1973. He came here during a cholera epidemic, but the plague did not spare him. We carried him out, dehydrated from vomiting and diarrhea. After him, I don't remember any other doctor visit."

"You think the angel can cure you, don't you?"

"Well, if not him, I don't know who."

Next was a gentleman with a dark bow tie and hair combed in an old-fashioned style: "Excuse me, sir, do you really think he's an angel?"

"It has been proven."

"How?"

"He shows up in my home. Not like here, in flesh and blood, but in his spiritual form. The first one to see him was my mother, God rest her soul, when she was in the kitchen ironing shirts. That afternoon my wife noticed she was talking to herself very softly, and asked if she needed anything. She replied, 'I am taking care of this angel of the Lord, who came to tell me that my time has come.' Since my mother was pointing to the corner where we have the gas tank, my wife looked and saw him too. It was a beautiful glow and you could feel the warmth. The brightness continued for a long time, and they stayed with him until he left so as not to offend him. Three days later my mother died. Since then, the angel visits us frequently. He always likes to come to the same corner, and there he glows and stays with us until he leaves."

To a boy in a black leather jacket: "You believe in all this?"

"It's better to believe than not to."

A lady with a handbag the color of Havana cigars and high-heeled shoes to match, confessed, "I'm here because I want to ask him for a home of my own."

"And you think he'll give it to you?"

"He granted one to a neighbor of mine, so why not to me?"

To a woman with a child in her arms: "Are you sure the Angel of Galilea is an angel and not a human being?"

"How can someone who knows so many languages be human?"

A fifteen-year-old girl: "I am here to ask him for a boyfriend. Well, I really have one already, but my family doesn't know yet."

"Then what is it you are asking for?"

"I want him to make my stepfather allow me to have a boyfriend."

An old man with colorless eyes: "I come to ask for justice

[5 1]

and vengeance against the murderers of my son, who are free out there, somewhere."

"And what can the angel do?"

"Stab them with his flaming sword."

A man about thirty said: "I think it's all a hoax."

"So why did you come?"

"Out of curiosity."

A man in a *ruana,* cap, and scarf: "He may not be the Archangel Michael, but he is our angel."

To a young woman kneeling in the mud, so devout that she seemed about to levitate, I asked, "What's the angel's name?"

"The day his name is known, that will be the end of the world."

Following Orlando around had made me heady with scents of incense in the breeze of seraphic wings, and I was happy to blend in again with this throng of dispossessed people seeking salvation in the last house of the last neighborhood. But where was my angel? What was he doing that kept him from showing up to receive so much love, to listen to so many pleas, to save us forever or finish us off, once and for all, with his enigmatic presence and that disconcerted look in his tender, unfathomable eyes.

Sister María Crucifija and Marujita de Peláez—always in her blue cape—appeared a few more times, with Sweet Baby Killer standing behind them, a loyal bodyguard looking like a benevolent orangutan. Shouting through her megaphone, Crucifija subdued the crowd and ordered everybody to return to their homes because, she announced, there would be no angel today.

Without rancor, the people from El Paraíso began their trip back, their torches extinguished, their sick exhausted, their children asleep in their arms, resigned to heaven's rejection. It had chosen not to send its messenger. Good news here and bad there, abundance today and deprivation tomorrow, that was fate's capricious way, and they had no right to make any demands otherwise. They did not expect much from this life, and they would wait patiently for the Hereafter.

"Disappointed?" I asked the one in the leather jacket.

"No problem," he replied. "If not today, maybe tomorrow."

The people from El Paraíso returned to their homes, and Orlando, who was falling asleep, went home too. I could not return to mine because, in the first place, it was very late and there was no transport; second, because I was supposed to be at the *Somos* editorial office the following day with an article and photos, which I still did not have; and third, because I wanted to read Ara's journals. Above all, I had to find a way to see the angel again. I decided to spend the night at his home.

Where would he sleep? Surely Doña Ara, who loved him so dearly, would not let him sleep outside, exposed to the cold. If he slept in the cave, I was doomed, because I was incapable of going all the way up there by myself, much less going in to look for him in the dark, provided that Sweet

Baby Killer, who probably guarded the entrance against unwanted visitors such as myself, did not break my neck first.

Ara was awake, waiting for me, watching the last soap opera of the evening on an old black-and-white television.

"The pilgrims left downhearted because they could not see him," I said. "They had brought their children and their sick. Why didn't he come out, Doña Ara?"

"That's the way my son is. Sometimes he wants to present himself, and sometimes he doesn't."

With delicate care she poked the fire, adding some coals, fetched a woolen stole out of mothballs to place over my shoulders, set a chair next to the stove for me, and brought me a plate of food I didn't dare refuse, although I was not hungry.

"Go ahead and read until sleep closes your eyes, Miss Mona, and then, if you wish, lie down on my bed. I can sleep on Crucifija's cot. She is so skinny, she hardly takes up any space."

Her hospitality was no surprise, even though she was extraordinarily generous. I took it as a complicity coming from the relief of sharing with someone such a heavy burden of love. Today I believe that Doña Ara already suspected then what was about to happen . . . I didn't know yet, but she did.

"Tell me, Doña Ara, where does your son spend the night?"

"I have never been able to get him to sleep on a bed. He doesn't like beds. He lies down on a straw mat on the floor, close to the stove, and he doesn't close his eyes. My son is strange, Miss Mona. When he is awake, he looks asleep, and when he is asleep, he seems to be awake."

"So he lives in twilight sleep . . . Are all angels like that?"

"They must be, with one eye on this world and the other on the mystery."

"Why isn't he here now?"

"Because of a disagreement with Crucifija. She doesn't always know how to handle him. He was restless, so I let him sleep in the yard, on the other side of that door."

My heart beat faster when I realized there was but a thin wooden board between that celestial creature and me. I dared ask his mother: "May I open the door?"

"Let's wait until Crucifija is completely asleep," she answered, lowering her voice.

"All right."

We could hear from the other room a murmur of slurred words, Crucifija's prayers.

"Sit down and read. Here." Doña Ara gave me the key to the trunk. "I'll watch the end of my soap opera."

"Doña Ara, one more little thing before you go . . . Tell me, what is your son's name?"

"He doesn't have a name yet. They took him away from me before I had time to give him a name. While he was away, I would cry out for him over and over, calling him only 'my boy, my little boy.' That father of mine never referred to him at all, and neither did my mother. Perhaps they thought that if they never mentioned him, I would forget him and forgive them. When the boy came back a man, I asked him many times. I did not want to impose my choice of a name on him, but to respect whatever name life had given him. So far, he has not told me."

I was thinking of my article. If the angel had no name, I would have to refer to him as "the Angel of Galilea," that was all. My boss wasn't going to like it; he would have preferred something more sensational, like Lucifer or Fulgur. Or in the worst of cases, Orifiel.

"Isn't his name Orifiel, Doña Ara?"

"Orifiel is only one of his masks. He does not reveal his real name. You should always mistrust angels who tell you their names."

"One last question. Is it true you dreamed of a calf?"

"Yes, it's true, but I meant no offense, least of all to Father Benito."

She sat on an armchair facing the television set, as circumspect and straight-backed as if she were at a funeral, and began watching the gray figures gesticulating in silence.

"Please turn the volume up, Doña Ara, it doesn't bother me."

"What for? I already know what they are going to say. You just go ahead and read in peace."

I inserted the key in the trunk padlock, with the awe of someone opening the Seventh Seal. I started to read the Revelations of the Fifty-Three Journals, caressing the parchmentlike and yellowed pages that so many licked fingers had turned over and over.

I undid my braid so that my hair, still damp, would finish drying in the warmth of the fire. I was not so much reading as trying to read, stunned by the beat of tom-toms resounding inside me.

What was it about this young man that so disturbed me? He was so fiercely handsome, enigmatic, and unreachable; more than a woman could take in and keep her composure.

I looked at my watch, waited an eternity, looked at it again; not even a quarter of an hour had gone by. The soap opera ended with the lovers parting.

"Really bad, really bad today," Doña Ara pronounced, turning the television off. "These television stars always have to suffer."

At that moment the clock struck twelve. My angel is going to turn into a pumpkin, I thought. Crucifija's mousy prayers had already quieted down; Ara spied on her through the crack of the partly open door.

"She looks dead rather than asleep," she said. "Now, Mona, now you can go into the yard."

In the meantime I had retrieved my camera. I would have liked to ask Doña Ara if she would let me use it, but I didn't because I was afraid she would say no. So I stuffed it in my shoulder bag, together with the oranges and the pants that I had bought at La Estrella.

"Are you coming with me, Doña Ara?"

"I better not. I'll wait here for you. If he frightens you, call me."

"Does he frighten people?"

"Sometimes, when he's startled."

The door had no lock, a little push was enough to open it,

and yet, my hand seemed unwilling to obey the commands of my brain. "I have to go out, there's just a boy out there," my mind was saying. But my heart was saying something else, and my feet remained glued to the floor. Finally, the urge to go out was stronger than the one to stay in, and I was able to walk through the door.

It was a small open yard, about nine feet by nine feet. And there he was, sitting against the washbasin, bathed in a fantastic beam of moonlight.

His head was thrown back, his gaze lost in the starlit night. He was slowly rocking back and forth, far away in some otherworldly dream, while his lips muttered unintelligible words.

He was there and, at the same time, he was not, and for a long time I just witnessed his autistic trance. Certain that he was unaware of me, I was able to scrutinize him to my heart's content, confirming that his inconceivable handsomeness was real. His thick, raven-wing hair, his dreamy eyes, shiny like velvet-black oil; the wistful fluttering of his dark lashes, his straight nose, his full and feminine lips from which broke forth, like smoke, the strange sounds of his hypnotic mantra. His swarthy, large body, like Michelangelo's David sculpted in dark marble, surrendered placidly to the powerful beam of light that connected him to the starry realm.

"Can you see me? Can you hear me?" I asked, raising my voice.

I could not break his isolation. I sat down near him, but he remained oblivious, on the other side of the invisible wall, godlike and inaccessible as a saint in his shrine, or a movie star on the screen. I gazed at him, enraptured by his radiant perfection, when suddenly I thought I noticed a gleam of cruelty in his absent stare. A fleeting shadow of absolute selfishness crossed over his face and made me shudder; just as soon it vanished and his face recovered its pure light, its pure peace.

I wanted to touch him. I reached out slowly, like someone trying to catch an unwilling animal, or wanting to pet a distrustful dog without getting bitten. My fingers touched him lightly and sizzled. He's burning with fever, I thought.

One by one I discovered his scars. On his thigh, a long, dark line, jagged as a mountain ridge; a broken line bisected his right eyebrow; another crossed his abdomen at the level of the appendix; a little relief map on his chest; an irregular star on his jaw; on his forearm, the unmistakable rosette of a smallpox vaccination; on his ankle, a recent scratch that had not yet shed its scab. They were evidence of the angel's passage through earthly pain. Who could have caused these wounds, who had disinfected them, who had stitched them?

"Who has hated you, angel? Who has loved you?" I asked. But he remained silent, like the scars on his body.

I don't know how, but I managed to remember *Somos*, the article, the photos. I took my camera, focused, and clicked. The flash caused the angel to start in reaction, as if hurt. I saw him cover his face with his arm, and it seemed to me he had suddenly fallen back into the real world, like a bird wounded in full flight or an astronaut landing on frigid ocean waters. He looked at me in bewilderment, and then stiffened and began to retreat with the grim caution of a beast escaping a hunter's ambush.

What could I do? He was huge, much taller than I, and he filled the space anxiously, like an eagle trapped in a canary cage. I feared his reaction; I felt cornered and helpless, and I wanted to flee. But then I realized he was more afraid of me than I was of him, and I recovered my self-control.

I had to calm down, calm him down, and communicate with him, now that he was finally awake and aware of me.

One approaches a scared animal by offering a piece of bread, and that is all I could think of. In a clumsy attempt, I took one of my oranges and threw it at his hands.

It worked. His reflexes kicked in and he caught the fruit. For a moment he forgot me and concentrated on the round, bright object that had fallen into his hands. He examined it carefully, and to my amazement, he smiled. It was a warm smile that instantly dissolved the light years separating us, an unexpected and magical bridge that allowed us to make contact.

The angel imitated my move. He threw the orange back at me, and I caught it and laughed. He was laughing too, with a tinkling adolescent laugh that could only belong to a happy angel. We engaged in this particular sport for one or two centuries, under the timeless radiance of the moon, until I hid the orange behind my back, which caused him to come closer, intrigued, in order to look for it. I started to peel the orange, and when done, I said "Eat," and offered it to him, but he made no move to take it. I put a section in my mouth while he was watching me. I took another section and held it close to his mouth.

That night he ate from my hand, one piece of fruit after another, section by section. My fingertips knew the warmth of his tongue; they can still recall the texture of his saliva.

The clothes I had bought for him, although extra large, were obviously too short and too tight. When he tired of the oranges, he went back to humming his strange tunes and took to playing with my hair, my extravagant mass of hair, golden like a fake coin and long like a virgin's mantle. It fascinated and attracted him, as it did all poor people. After all, my angel, dispossessed and naked, was one of them.

Dawn approached our patch of open sky over the yard, and I suddenly remembered Ara, who would still be awake and waiting for me. My God! How could I? I had forgotten all about her, about my own self, and about everything else. For hours my heart and mind had belonged to him, my mythological creature, my beautiful galactic animal. My archangel of Galilea.

Falling under his spell I had lost myself in the unreal world of his dream, and together we had flown far away from that yard into the boundless universe of his detachment. And now, completely against my will, I had to return.

As soon as I opened the door, I felt the wrench. With one gesture I had brutally torn myself from him, breaking the thinnest of bonds, one which perhaps I could never repair. I wished I could change my mind and return, but it was too late.

All at once, the angel had cloistered himself again into the impassive coldness of a statue, and again his eyes, although they looked at me, didn't see me anymore.

Woman who comes near me, do not wish to know my name. For you I am the Angel Without a Name: I cannot tell you my name, nor could you pronounce it.

I knew you would come from below, and I was waiting for you, for it was written that the city would send you to me. With the same yearning that the earth, shivering in darkness, awaits the redeeming splendor of the sun—that is how I have waited for you. And now that you are here, I do not know you.

I wish to come near you, I stretch out my hand to touch you. But your skin is fire and it burns me; I do not know how to bear the intense pain of your touch. Do not speak to me, do not look at me. Your words bewilder me, and your gaze, unbearably, pierces my eyes.

But do not move away. Too much closeness to you suffocates me, and too much distance kills me. I see your hair undulating on the other side, the mass of your hair that floats and fills all the space. Your unfathomable body terrifies me, I flee from those hands of yours that want to grasp me. But the blond cloud of your hair beckons me generously and encourages me to come out of the cold and to bury myself in the music of its golden revelry. Your hair does not frighten me because it grew outside of you and no longer belongs to you, it accompanies me but does not entrap me, it brushes against my skin but does not burn me. I touch your hair and feel no pain.

Do not persist in trying to find out my name. Perhaps I have no name, and if I do, it is manifold and ever changing. My name, my names: fleeting, misleading, full of different echoes. In your world there are no ears that could perceive their frequency, and no eardrums that could withstand their resonance.

Do not wish to talk to me: your words are noise. They come to me in fragments, like shards of broken glass. They hurt me, make me bleed, and they tell me nothing.

Do not try to love me: your love destroys me.

Do not expect me to love you: I am not of this place, I am not here. I am trying to find my way here, and I fail.

Your presence torments me: it is too oppressive. Your weight shatters my wings and unleashes my fears.

Your hair, in contrast, welcomes me joyfully and I find refuge in it. Its sunny strands tickle me, make me laugh. Do not move away. Do not touch me. Do not get too close, but do not leave. Have infinite patience with me, because infinite is the number of days that I have waited for you.

Let your hair shelter me, become my mantle, a rush of sheep through meadows of golden light. Rescue me from my ambiguous existence, from the haze that envelops me. Clear this cloudy substance, made out of distance and silence, that clings to my senses and blurs them, that invades my innermost being and suffocates me. Let the warm light of your hair envelop me, and cast away shadows.

Elohim, Fallen Angel

THAT IS ALL THAT HAPPENED THAT NIGHT IN THE YARD. SOME people may think it was nothing much; they simply do not understand, because they never had an angel sing to them in Aramaic while he caressed their hair.

I went back inside, but could not find Doña Ara; probably, seeing that it was useless to wait for me any longer, she had gone to bed.

I lay down fully clothed, shaken, exhausted, thinking of resting for only a few minutes, but I slept soundly until late that morning.

When I opened my eyes and tried to get up, the memory of the angel thrust me back like a powerful wave. It completely took me by surprise to find myself in this condition, overwhelmed by an extraordinary passion for the anonymous young man in the backyard.

My colleagues have always accused me of lacking professionalism because of my inability to maintain the appropriate objectivity and distance from my subjects. On one occasion I went on assignment for eight days to Nicaragua, to cover the conflict between the Sandinistas and the Contras, and I ended up staying there, deeply involved in their struggle, on the side of the Sandinistas. When I was covering the Armero volcano tragedy with a television news crew, before I knew it, I had adopted one of its victims, an old lady who had lost everything, even her memory. She has been living in my home ever since, convinced that she is my aunt. Now I had proven my colleagues right again, and this time it was pathetic: I had been sent to search for an angel; I had not only found him, I had also fallen in love with him.

I did not have to look at the empty yard to know that he was no longer there. A palpable absence in the air hinted at his departure. I was going to say good-bye to Ara and return to the city, to *Somos,* to deliver the photos I had taken the previous day—especially the only one I had managed to take of him—and to write my first article on one of the obsolete computers in the editorial office. I would then return to Galilea in the afternoon to continue my investigation. Now that the angel was mine, I had to find out, once and for all, who he was, where he came from, and, above all, where he was going.

I could not leave as quickly as I intended because I got involved in a conflict that caused a commotion in the household. Hostility between Doña Ara and María Crucifija was evident in the silence of one and the noisy clatter of the other, who was banging dishes and pots, along with every other object she could lay her hands on.

It's all my fault, I thought. The word has got out that I spent the night with the angel, and they are upset. This is my typical way of thinking: Whenever I fall in love, I am racked by guilt and the compulsion to apologize. But when Doña Ara came to my room with my breakfast, I gave her a questioning look, and she patted my head as if telling me not to worry, that the problem had nothing to do with me.

Through certain sharp phrases, Crucifija led me to understand the reason for the discord. It seems that the previous evening, while the pilgrims from El Paraíso were waiting outside, Crucifija had committed an unforgivable sin: tired of summoning the angel politely, she had tried to tie a rope around him to make him come out. Now, while Ara was serving me scrambled eggs with onions and tomatoes, Sister Crucifija tried to shift the responsibility for the problem to her.

"You indulge him in everything," the sister was screaming, "and the only thing you accomplish is that the boy pretends he doesn't understand. Because he doesn't want to understand that he too has responsibilities . . ."

"Don't you abuse my boy," Ara kept saying, her voice quivering with resentment.

When Crucifija walked away, Doña Ara, her eyes filled with tears, said, "Oh, Mona, I heard last night how you made him laugh. Thank you, Monita. You woke my son up and made him happy!"

"We haven't won the battle yet, Ara," I warned her.

The conflict was reduced to a mere temporary misunderstanding, in the face of the bad news that Marujita de Peláez brought in from the outside world. She arrived, all excited, to inform us that Father Benito had declared war from the pulpit that morning against María Crucifija. He had left her no way out, demanding that if she were a nun, she had to start acting like one; she had to leave town and join a convent. Those attending mass left church agitated and yelling, "The nun to the nunnery!" and showing their determination to take her there, even if they had to drag her by the hair.

It so happened that Father Benito, alarmed by the size of the dissident procession the day before, had decided to change his strategy. Up until now, his campaign had been tentative, directed sometimes against the angel, with the allegation that he was an impostor, and at other times against Ara, simply for being his mother. But Ara was too much of a solitary, suffering figure for him to be able to arouse a cohesive, belligerent opposition. Father Benito did not believe that the young man was an angel; on the contrary, he was convinced that the youth was a demon. And Father Benito was so afraid of this demon that, although he would assail him with virulent tirades, he did not dare try to convert any of his verbal attacks into direct action.

Sister Crucifija, however, was a more vulnerable target. It was important to stop her because she had become a sinister female pope challenging Father Benito's spiritual authority and assembling crowds of the faithful in open defiance of the official Church's proscription of the angel. The heresy was spreading, gaining followers and, as the crowning insult, it was led by a woman.

Crucifija, Marujita, Sweet Baby Killer, and the other councilwomen declared a state of emergency and rushed into closed quarters for deliberations, so I had a chance to speak privately with Ara.

I was eager to talk to her about her son, but I learned little. When I asked if her son had perhaps suffered a head injury when he was a child, or suggested possible mental problems, Ara was deaf to any such hypotheses, and would close the matter by simply asserting that he was an angel.

"Certainly he is an angel," I assented, "but you yourself agreed that it would be good to 'wake him up.' That he is a strange youth. Or rather, that he is not normal . . ."

"Who said angels were normal?" she retorted. That was the extent of our debate.

About Sister María Crucifija, however, we gossiped to our hearts' content.

The story of her leadership had not started yesterday, it dated from before the appearance of the angel, whose veneration she now directed.

Crucifija's charismatic power had its origins in her escape from the flames on the day of the 1965 fire, when Galilea was not yet the popular neighborhood it is today, but a steep, uninhabited cliff occupied only by a spectral convent with thirty-four cloistered nuns.

The high walls and the hermetically closed doors made the outside world suspect that real women no longer lived there, only spirits. This belief was confirmed daily from dawn till the evening Angelus by their ethereal chanting, like the song of sirens, seeping out through the cracks, rising into the winds, and causing apprehension among the few inhabitants of the neighboring regions. The belief, however, was contradicted by the black waters flowing downhill from the pipes of the convent, loaded with quite material, human excrement.

Nobody knows how this famous fire started, but it did not end until the very stones were scorched and thirty-three of the sisters were turned to dust, as well as all the animals in the stables and corrals, the geraniums in the flowerpots, the greens in the vegetable gardens, and even the pigeons, so well fed that they were too fat to fly.

The only living being to escape this hell on earth was the youngest of the novices, an ill-tempered and rebellious orphan who had not yet taken her vows but who had already been given the initiate name of María Crucifija.

She herself would never mention this event, but legend had it that the people watching the disaster saw her emerge from the flames miraculously unscathed, with the exception of singed lashes and eyebrows that never grew back, giving her the ghastly appearance of a Martian, or the naked look of a guava worm.

Nobody knew for sure who Sister María Crucifija was, but everybody knew very well who she was not. You could not truthfully state that she was a woman. She rather belonged to a third sex, of those who have given up sex forever.

She was not a nun, but an ascetic by her own choosing. She had taken chastity and poverty vows—though the latter didn't count, if you consider that the whole population of Galilea was dirt poor without having to take any vows.

Sister María Crucifija was intact, not only in the symbolic sense that she was a virgin, but in the strictly literal sense of the word: no man had ever touched her. Her aversion to the flesh was so intense that she had even managed to make it disappear from her own body: her anorexic thinness had made her into a fleshless being, a mere spiritual bundle of bones wrapped in skin.

She did not allow even a hint of color in her clothes, but her mourning was not attributable to the loss of family or loved ones, since she was not known to have any. It was more an act of contrition for women being to blame for original sin.

This life of renunciation had both helped and hindered her. The advantage was that, in spite of not being a man, it had granted her a considerable measure of power in the neighborhood. The disadvantage was that it had made her a challenge to the natural order of things and, therefore, an easy target for attacks. In the morning sermon, for example, Father Benito had blamed her—along with her creation, the angel—for the disastrous rainfall that was threatening to sweep Galilea away; for the seven cases of hepatitis that had arisen during the preceding month; and even for a chicken born with two heads, a phenomenon that had upset the whole community.

Ara interrupted her story to prepare food for the angel.

"What does he eat?" I asked her.

"Bread. Angel bread."

I almost told her I was going with her, so I could get to see him and hand-feed him crumb by crumb, but my sense of duty was stronger. So we said good-bye, and I was about to leave for the city, when the deliberating council members came out of their seclusion and blocked my way. I was not going anywhere, Crucifija told me, because she had other plans for me.

"You must allow us to wash your hair," she said very solemnly, "with chamomile tea, which will lighten it. The end of the world has come, and we have to get moving!"

"Why wash my hair, if the world is coming to an end? Besides," I tried to defend myself, "it's clean."

She grabbed a tuft to check.

"It has split ends," she diagnosed, and without further ado, started to busy herself with pots of hot water. Since I had no interest whatsoever in having my split ends treated, I left some money on the table to pay for my meal, plus a little extra, and fled through the door.

Down the street ran Sister María Crucifija until she caught up with me.

"Where do you think you're going?" she yelled. "You can't leave!"

"Why not?"

"Because we are all depending on you."

"Don't get excited, I'll be back later."

"When you come back, it'll be too late."

"Too late for whom?"

"For the angel. For all of us. For the human race. Even for you . . ."

"I'm sorry, but I have to submit an article."

"Look, if you don't want to, you don't have to wash your hair. All you have to do is give a message to the angel. He listens to you . . ."

Those were the magic words. She said them and I surrendered: If I could see the angel, I would stay. And I would even wash my hair, since he had liked it so much. So I agreed to Crucifija's request on the condition that she would give me an hour to write my report and provide me with a messenger to deliver it.

And thus on that day, on my second day in Galilea, Doña Ara and Marujita de Peláez—armed with warm water, chamomile extract, a pair of Fuller brushes, and one of those old-fashioned dryers that look like an astronaut's helmet—installed me in the backyard, took charge of my mass of hair, and worked away at it until it glowed.

Step by step, from the trivial to the insignificant, you get to the definitive. Obviously nobody attaches any importance to a hair washing, unless it is a step in the preparation of a ritual.

Do you hear the murmur, do you feel the light touch?

Shhhh . . . Don't be afraid. It is I who approaches you, I, Gabriel, the Archangel of Annunciations. I have come down to whisper the good news to you. Don't you recognize me? There is no mistaking me, look at me closely. None other has his body covered with saffron-colored hair or topaz green wings, or the bright sun shining between his eyes. It's me, Gabriel, of the one million tongues . . . Listen to them whispering my message in your ear.

"Scat!" you shout, shooing me away as if I were a cat. And I hide behind the wardrobe and stay there for hours, crouching

in the semidarkness, waiting for you to calm down, or to fall asleep.

"Scat!" you shout again as soon as I try to get closer. Quiet, woman, don't be skittish. Don't give me away. You don't know what awaits me for having come to you! I shudder at the divine warning that still resounds in the air. It has been proclaimed since the day of creation, and of all forbidden acts, this is the one God punishes most severely. There is no angel or archangel, throne or authority, virtue or power that is not aware of the consequences of his terrible anger.

This is what Yahweh said, with the voice that expelled Satan. "The angel who dares go down to earth to unite with a woman shall forfeit his eternal life."

We angels listened to Him, felt fear and the desire to obey, and for centuries remained chaste. But the day came when some of us were in a position to behold closely the daughters of men, to witness their beauty and the sweetness of their ways, and, no longer able to resist temptation, descended to Earth, looked for the women, and made love to them.

The Lord, who knows everything, learned about this too. The skies lit up with his fury, and his terrible dictum thundered throughout the seven galaxies. "You, holy and spiritual angels, blessed with the gift of eternal life, you have sullied yourselves with the blood of women, you have engendered life with the blood of the flesh; as only human blood does, you have lusted, and you have made flesh and blood like those who die and perish."

Among the fallen were Harut and Marut, beautiful and strong, favorites of the Lord, each of whom had exchanged eternity for a moment of passion with a woman, as did Lucifer, knowing full well what he was giving up, as much as what he had to gain.

The punishment they received, and that of the two hundred others who were with women, was permanent isolation in deep caves, for their sin was against nature, that is, against their own nature as angels, which is pure and uncontaminated and does not require carnal union to perpetuate itself.

But even more horrendous was the punishment meted out to the women they loved, because the Lord, in his anger, blamed the women for their seductions, and condemned them to be repudiated as prostitutes, and then, stripped of their clothes, chained, and abandoned until their sin is fully atoned for in the year of mystery.

Since then, it is well known that the Lord does not trust women, though they are his own creation, and considers them the vessels of filth and sin. And it is His will that the angels in heaven, as well as the saints on earth, distance themselves from women, as the first requirement to protect their virtue. Because it will be easier for a camel to pass through the eye of a needle than for a woman to enter the kingdom of heaven, unless she is a mother or a virgin, and the greatest of them all, who sits on a throne next to the Son, will miraculously be mother as well as virgin, and both at the same time. The one who is only a woman will not know forgiveness, because she will be considered filth, her blood contagious, and her entire body wicked. As the prophet so well said: "You would have to be a woman to know what it means to be scorned by God."

Woe is me, Gabriel, the messenger! The Archangel, red as

glowing embers, hairy as a lamb! Until yesterday, I was playing the zither, innocent and blinded by God's splendor. Today I have seen you, and I have found you beautiful, and I have found you good, clean, and luminous. Desire entangles me more fervently than guilt, and it is my last will to make you mine.

I am well aware that there are not enough tears to pay for such a sin. That in punishment I will lose my name and will be called Elohim, which means "Fallen Because He Sinned with Woman Dragging Humanity Down into Corruption and the Whole World Toward the Flood." And yet here I am, and I do not weaken. I come near you, step by step, and I am still Gabriel, even though my name today is Elohim. Listen, woman, to my message, because mine are words of love.

The decision has been made. I, Gabriel Elohim, son of the heavens, will meld with you, daughter of men, like one wine and another wine when poured together into the same wineskin.

Do not flee, woman, and do not be afraid. Come into the cave with me, where springs of clear water flow, where nard gives forth its fragrance, and aloe fruit, pepper, and cinnamon fill the air. There we shall take refuge from God's unmerciful eyes. There I will make you mine, you, my blessed one, my beloved, my only one, and plant my seed within you.

Within each other we will have the joy of living and also the joy, unknown to me, of dying. Together we shall penetrate epiphanies and obscurities, we shall rise to the pinnacle and fall into the abyss, and I shall be happy because I shall finally understand that all that is real has a beginning, and that it ends and is extinguished when it has no more reason for being.

I shall sit at the edge of the world to behold you, woman, and in shy modesty I shall cover my eyes with my wings before the beauty of your face. I shall look at you and have my fill of you because he who looks is infused by that which he sees.

Holding your hand I will roam all corners of the world of the senses, which for angels is forbidden by the will of God. Through you I shall know the pleasures of seeing, hearing, smelling, touching, and of carnal love, which are solely human prerogatives. For an instant I shall possess pleasure and pain, and marble, chinaberries, fragrances. Forgetting and remembering will also be mine. And mine shall be bread, as well as wine, oil, sickness, and health. Through you I shall know the secrets of science and of the arts, I shall know agriculture, metallurgy, poetry, the alphabet, the numbers, the dyeing of textiles, the art of applying antimony. To enjoy all of that is a privilege that must be paid for by death, and I am willing to pay the price.

In exchange, I will open the doors to your inner temple and let your eyes behold the mysteries. I will put in your hands, woman, the ineffable mystery that God has made available only to priests and hierophants. You shall roam the skies on my back, and you shall see the foundations of the universe, the cornerstone of the Earth, the four columns of Heaven, the secrets of time that becomes space and can be traveled forward or backward, the places where the wind hides, the plains where clouds graze, the mounds that hoard hail, the huge pools where rain is waiting . . .

After the union, the time of reproduction will come.

Do you know, woman, how angels reproduce? The wise holy men cannot come to an agreement. Some believe it is by some kind of disintegration, as mercury does. Or like a mirror, which *shatters into fragments that reflect one another. Saint Thomas, the Angelic Doctor, claims we reproduce like flies. None of that has any importance because when the time comes, things will be as they should be.*

When the day comes, we shall see the clear signs in the sky, we shall interpret them, and we shall know that because of our actions the prophecy will be fulfilled, because it is written that when angels descend from heaven, their race and that of the daughters of men will become one.

But before all is done, our time of parting will come. The ancient warnings will be realized. You will hear these words: "Ave, woman, we are both full of grace, I have been in you, and you have been in me." You will recognize in them my voice, and in my voice, our farewell, and you will cry, because I shall be gone.

And now, do you hear the rustle? Do you feel the touch? Shhh . . . Be quiet, woman, keep silent, do not shout and alarm others in your house. Don't be afraid, I do not want to startle or terrify you, I am just a fallen angel. Leave the door open, for it is I, Elohim, and I am afire with passion.

I knew I was about to see him and was overcome by such burning anxiety as I had never experienced before and probably never will again. How can I describe that morning, the best of my life, except to say that a newly born sun shone into the yard, that water was spluttering from the tap, and that the air was filled with the joy of women busy at their work.

I let Ara and Marujita comb my hair, and get me ready any way they pleased, and in the meantime, I thought only of

him. I don't know at what point they changed my clothes
and dressed me in a long blue tunic, suitable for a virgin or
a madwoman, depending on how you looked at her, and got
me up on some kind of palanquin or portable platform, as if
I were a religious statue in the Holy Week procession. I do
not know exactly when all this happened, and I did not care;
they had absolute confidence in me as an enthusiastic and
unconditional accomplice. By the time I came to realize it,
we were already in the street, and more and more people
were arriving, crowding around me because, apparently, I
was the center of attention.

My eyes searched for others dressed in blue tunics like
mine, but everyone else was in street clothes; I was the only
one in costume. This discouraged me, and I looked for Orlando. Where on earth was Orlando, my friend, my inter-
preter, my guide? Where had he gone that he was no longer
here to help me, now that I had become the star of this
whole production? Ara told me that the boy was doing his
homework, that he went to school in the mornings.

I was at the crest of the wave of these events, and there was
no possibility of my turning back. The councilwomen
planted a crown of flowers on my head, placed a bouquet in
my hands, spread my hair out like a mantle, and installed on
my shoulders the ostentatious and stunning blue cape of
Marujita de Peláez.

Sweet Baby Killer and three strong men shouldered the
platform with me on top, and in order not to fall, I had to
drop the bouquet and hang on to the contraption's low rail-

ing. And so, on human shoulders, I moved over the heads of the crowd like a beauty queen on a parade float.

A swarm of people milled around me, this time mostly women and infants. Sister Crucifija, who wanted order, tried hard to line them up and handed out mimeographed sheets with the hymns that were to be sung.

As we moved down through Barrio Bajo, more of the faithful left their homes to join the procession. They followed me, the living statue heading the parade. My four carriers often slipped on the still-soft mud, the platform tilted dangerously, and I rode along as if on a roller coaster, hanging on for dear life to avoid landing in the mud. The devout gave me looks of love and admiration, which seemed excessive to me. I started to wake from the spell and wanted to get down from that absurd thing, and I would have done it, if at that very moment I had not seen him.

Another group in another procession was carrying him, also on a palanquin. We were heading downhill, and the angel and his entourage were coming uphill, so we would meet midway. His body was covered with an ample white cloth, which billowed in the wind like a triumphal cloak and allowed glimpses of his powerful arms and the swarthy skin of his chest and back.

He was smiling like someone miraculously brought to life from the dead, or a triumphant crusader celebrating his victory over the Moors, and in the midst of the rush of horses bolting inside my chest, I saw him as larger than life, an invincible and celestial figure. On that day, I swear, the angel was weightless. As he approached and went by me, his body was brimming with physical power and overflowing with grace. His hair radiated a special glow, and there was fire in his eyes. Seeing his full glory on display, I understood the secret of his impressive presence: he looked utterly human but he was made of light, not of earthly dust.

His presence gave meaning to the surrounding chaos. Superstition became ritual; the grotesque, sacred. As if following orders, the way a metal particle seeks the magnet, I let myself be pulled behind him, anonymous, yielding, one among the many mortals, asking no questions and offering no resistance.

Led by a group of kids brandishing small jars with incense, the procession started its uphill climb, leaving the neighborhood behind and entering the thicket, carrying us in the open litters on their shoulders, first the angel in all his splendor, then me, totally enraptured.

The angel had also been crowned with flowers. The procession clambered up; the *carbonero* and *guapanto* bushes became more and more entangled, the ferns gigantic, and the blackberries were everywhere. The sky seemed so close you could almost touch it, and the city, way down below, looked unreal. Where were they taking us, so far, so high? I did not care, as long as I was with him.

I doubt whether I should describe what happened next, for I'm not sure I'll be able to make it credible. It will sound crazy and foolish at best, but it was not that at all. Exactly the opposite. Today, so many years later, I am convinced it was the most complete and lucid act of my life.

After reaching a cross erected on the highest point of the cliff, where offerings were made, we descended again to the caves called Bethel Grottoes, where I had seen him for the first time the previous afternoon. At the entrance, Sister María Crucifija stopped the procession and, standing on a rock, delivered a sermon about the end of the world, the need for pairing, the final hours that were already counted, and the great mission of the people of Galilea, on whose shoulders Heaven had seen fit to place the responsibility of the gestation of the new angel, the one who would come down to earth to replace his predecessor, so that the link that started with Jesus would not be broken.

Up until then, the ceremony had been strange, but the oddest moment was yet to come. Sister Crucifija grabbed an out-of-tune treble guitar, which someone handed to her, and with a nun's voice that would scare just about anybody, started to sing, of all things, the popular wedding folk song, "White and radiant comes the bride, followed by her loving bridegroom . . . ," hammering away at the low notes and introducing some changes in the words in order to make it less pagan. The people clapped and accompanied her with tambourines, and even a pair of maracas, which kept their own, independent rhythm. It was a dissonant concert, each person with his or her own interpretation. It sounded rather like a satanic hymn.

Some people embraced, overcome by emotion: Marujita and Sweet Baby Killer were crying. And I? Did I understand what it all meant, and what role had been assigned to me? Did I know what was to come? It was pretty obvious. It did not require any brains to figure out why yesterday Sister Crucifija had inquired about the dates of my period, why Doña Ara was so affectionate toward me, or to explain the blue tunic, my place of honor, my clean hair.

From the moment I appeared in the neighborhood, the councilwomen had elected me. They found me to be the appropriate one, the so-long-hoped-for white and radiant bride, the one who, because of being tall, or having blond hair, or perhaps because I came from the outside, had the ideal qualifications to procreate with the angel. Nothing had been left to chance, and Father Benito's offensive had only hastened the moment.

And myself, I could only gaze at him; his presence stunned me, left me in a trance. I venerated only him. And I wanted him.

"Do unto me according to your will," I would have said, if such a statement was not heresy, and if he had been able to ask me.

The pilgrims stopped singing and returned to the Barrio, leaving us alone, just the two of us, in the fresh morning breeze. I was burning with excitement, trembling, empty of all but desire. I looked at him, and only one throbbing thought crossed my mind: Whatever will be, let it be.

And so it was. Inside the grotto the angel made love to me with the instinct of an animal, the passion of a man, and the furor of a god.

He took me as I am, a whole woman. With all of me he made his sanctuary, forgetting neither my heart nor my womanhood, the longings of my soul nor the desires of my flesh. He delighted in my sacred, pure love and drank of my profane, carnal passion, nor was he afraid of the total abandon with which I gave myself, flowing in a torrent, and overflowing both the boundaries and the source.

Our union was a sacrament.

Holy is my soul and holy is my body, with true love I joyfully accept both. Holy is maternity and holy is sexuality, holy the penis and holy the vagina, holy is pleasure and blessed is orgasm, because they are clean and pure and holy, and they shall inherit the kingdoms of Heaven and Earth, because they have suffered persecution and calumny. Let them be praised now because before they were called unmentionable. Blessed forever be the sin of the flesh, when it is committed with so much passion and so much love.

After that day nothing was ever the same. An open wound in my heart: that and no less was the story of my love for the Angel of Galilea. His tender sweetness had made me lose my mind, his mystery and his silence had totally undone me. My time stood still and I began living in his, which had nothing to do with clocks. My soul opened to the sudden gust of intense winds coming from afar. That morning in the grotto I discovered my heart bleeding inside, drip, drip, drip, red drops trickling down from my heart. The source of my joy and of my sorrow had come to me all at once. I am ashamed to say this, it just isn't said anymore, but I confess that I felt for him the agonies of a heart that burns and bleeds for love.

Mermeoth, or the Fury of the Angel

THERE IS NO HIGHER DRAMA IN MY CITY THAN THE SEARCH FOR A public telephone. If you do find one, the handset has been ripped off, and if there is a handset, the dial is missing. People do strange things in telephone booths: they shit, write subversive slogans, explode bombs—everything except make phone calls. In Galilea, where there are no private phones, the two public ones had been ripped apart. Orlando walked with me to a bakery in a nearby neighborhood, where there was rumored to be a telephone in working order.

When I finally got through to my boss, he gave me an earful, demanding to know where I was and if I thought I was on vacation; he complained that the article I sent him was unpublishable garbage: What on earth was I thinking?

"And the photo of the angel?" I dared ask. "How was it?"

"What? Angel? You mean that big black smudge?"

"What about my article, didn't you like it?"

"No good. Can't you see? It's only poor people's superstitions, of no interest to anybody!"

I had to go down to *Somos* and whip something up or else they'd fire me. So we returned to Galilea, and Orlando walked me to the only corner where I might be able to catch a bus. On our way there, two things happened.

First, a few huge drops of rain started falling. I thought nothing of it then, but Orlando was very concerned.

"What's wrong?" I asked him. "Didn't it rain cats and dogs yesterday?"

"This rain is different."

"What makes it different?"

"This is the beginning of the Great Flood."

"Says who?"

"The Muñís sisters said this morning that when the rain began today, it would never stop."

"And who are the Muñís sisters?"

"Rufa and Chofa, two sisters from the neighborhood. They make jams and marmalade."

"What do they know about rain?"

"They know a lot about prophecies, even prophecies that only the Pope knows but doesn't want to reveal yet, like the ones about the little shepherds of Fatima."

"How did the Muñís sisters learn such secrets?"

"The Sáenz women told them."

"And what prophecies are those?"

"The Muñís sisters have only revealed one. Well, really, only one of the sisters, Chofa Muñís, who has a big mouth.

Nobody can get a word out of Rufa, but Chofa jabbers on and on to anybody. You only have to tell her, 'You two don't know beans about anything,' and she feels stung in her pride and starts to sing. The other day she revealed one of the prophecies."

"Which one?"

"The fall of communism."

"Big deal."

At that point, the Muñís sisters' prediction did not seem convincing, but a few hours later, a downpour of biblical proportions made me credit their sibylline powers. Even though the disappearance of Galilea, swept away by the rains, would be as easy to predict as the fall of communism.

The other thing Orlando and I encountered was a couple of fresh graffiti on the walls, both signed with the initials D.T.F.A. One read: "The angel is a bastard," which actually revealed nothing, aside from the increasing level of hostility in the neighborhood. The other graffiti made Orlando furious; with my help, he kicked the wall and spat on it. It read: "Orlando is Father Benito's son."

Orlando, the son of Don Benito, the priest? He was so outraged that I asked him casually, as if changing the topic, "And, what's your mother's name?" But he wouldn't give me a straight answer. Soon the bus arrived. Through the bus window I saw Orlando still standing in the rain, now coming down faster in large drops.

When I got to *Somos* it was pouring. I will not describe my less-than-triumphant entrance because it's hardly worth it. I will only say that for me it was like a descent into another world, and that while I pined for my angel, who by now seemed as painfully remote as if I had met him on another planet, the editor in chief was tearing up my article. He showed me that the famous photograph was in fact a blur, and ordered me to redo everything for the following day. The subject could not be changed because the cover of the magazine's next issue had already been printed—the headline announcing, as I had anticipated, "Angels Alight in Colombia!" This time he sent me first to interview Marilú Lucena, a giant of the small screen who had been rescued by an angel as she returned home alone from a party, when her car broke down on a dark street at three in the morning.

Though the rain was still coming down in buckets, flooding several streets and causing major traffic jams even by Bogotá standards, after Marilú Lucena's confessions I had to visit one of our national senators, who assured me that as a child he had drowned and remained at the bottom of a swimming pool for more than two hours. He was here now to tell the story, he insisted, only because a group of angels had rescued him and returned him to life.

Around nine in the evening, during the worst downpour I had ever experienced, I went to the hotel where the bullfighter Gitanillo de Pereira was staying. In an exclusive interview for *Somos*, he told me that when he saw a little blue angel standing between the horns of a bull, he knew he was protected and nothing would happen to him.

About eleven, exhausted and totally fed up, I got back to my apartment, took a long-awaited shower in water hot enough to scald chickens, and had tea and sandwiches prepared by my aunt (the Armero volcano victim). At midnight when I was finally ready to sit down and transcribe the afternoon's revelations, the desk phone rang.

It was the night watchman from *Somos* saying that a boy was asking for me. The watchman had lied to him, following the magazine policy to ensure the privacy of its staff members, and said he didn't have my phone number. But the boy was so insistent and seemed so desperate that the watchman had felt sorry for him and decided to call me, just in case it was a real emergency.

"The boy says his name is—"

"Orlando," I interrupted. "Put him on quickly, please."

Orlando sounded confused and talked so fast I could hardly understand him. I gave him the address of my apartment, told him the watchman would help him get a taxi, and said I would pay for it when he got to my building.

When Orlando arrived, shaken and bleary-eyed, he did not even want to take off his wet shoes or have a hot chocolate. He said it was an emergency, that he had come for me, and that we had to return to Galilea right away because, as he said, "It's being dragged into Judgment Day."

"But what can we do there at this time of night?"

"Come on, Mona, you've got to come," he kept repeating as he pulled me by the sleeve.

"All right, Orlando, let's think this over. Sit down a minute and tell me exactly what's going on."

"It's the water. It's going to drag the houses down."

"Then let's call the firemen, the Disaster Prevention Center, someone who could help us avoid a catastrophe. Let me think where we could call . . ."

"No, Mona, no, they can't do anything. You're the only one who can."

"Me? With this rain, we probably can't even get there."

"You're the only one who can."

"Me? How?"

"By appeasing the angel. He's the one who's causing all the trouble."

"He? What did he do?"

"Remember I told you about the terrible angel? Well, that's it! The terrible angel is attacking again, see, and in his fury he's going to destroy the world . . ."

"Attacking again? What does that mean?"

"He's throwing a fit."

"What kind of a fit?"

"Well, it's like he gets struck by lightning, and it throws him against the wall like a rag doll, and his back arches in a huge curve, and then he gets so strong that not even Sweet Baby can hold him down, and he shits on himself and froths at the mouth, and his eyes turn red, bursting with blood, and . . ."

Orlando was describing an epileptic seizure, with all the colorful details and exaggerated precision common to the poor when they talk about illness. It was also giving me a fit, but of anguish and guilt. "I knew it, I knew it," I kept repeating angrily to myself. This young man, the love of my life, was sick, and it could have been prevented, but I was so far away, I couldn't help him, and worst of all, why was I so complacent, so absorbed in the magic and reassuring aspects of the angel, while the only reality now was his screaming, his convulsions battering his body against the ground, the nerve cells in his brain exacerbated to the point of delirium, his pupils turned inward trying to find the switch to turn off the turmoil in his head?

"Does he have these fits often?"

"Yes, plenty. And getting worse all the time."

I thought of Harry Puentes, my friendly next-door neighbor, who was just out of med school and had never refused me a favor. Perhaps he'd agree to take us to Galilea in his Mitsubishi four-wheel drive, lending us some moral support along the way.

Although we awakened him at that late hour, Harry graciously agreed to drive us. He pulled a sweater over his pajamas, put on a pair of hiking boots, and then the three of us took off into the night. As we drove on the solitary city bypass, Harry and I became nervous because in those days there were people who would lay logs across the road to stop vehicles. When they were in a good mood, they would get the occupants out and let them continue on foot, after giving them a good dose of scopolamine. Harry kept a gun in his glove compartment, but both of us also knew that, at the moment of truth, face-to-face with the mini-Uzis of professional highway robbers, the only thing we could do with our little pistol was shove it.

Luckily, the night was lit up by lightning, scaring away

even the criminals, so nobody bothered us, and no logs blocked our way. Although we did everything humanly possible to get up to Galilea through the various access roads, the jeep kept skidding, buffeted by gusts of wind, and rocking in the mud like a drunken ship. It was an impossible feat, even for three stubborn souls and four-wheel drive.

Through the fogged car windows we could see the storm pounding the mountains with a rage so violent it seemed human.

"It's the Seven Blows of God's Fury," Orlando said, shaking with fear.

"It's just a severe storm," I said, trying to calm him, although I seemed already to be hearing legions of angels blowing their trumpets full blast, sounding the final call to Judgment Day.

"Look at that! Don't you see it?" Orlando shouted, when a majestic flash of lightning unleashed its voltage on the ground.

"What?"

"Over there! Huge! With his head touching the sky!" Orlando yelled, beside himself.

"Calm down, kid," Harry said. "Tell me what you're seeing."

"I see Mermeoth, the Angel of Storms. Mermeoth has power over all the rivers, all the oceans, the drops of rain and even all the tears—all of the earth's waters. That's what Ara's journals say. Mermeoth is up there, and he's real mad! Look! His head is swallowing up bolts of lightning!"

"Let's go back," Harry said. "It's almost five in the morning, and we can't do anything for the young man up there. Instead, this boy here is going nuts on us."

We returned to my apartment and I thanked Harry for his efforts by making him a good breakfast. Then Orlando and I were left alone. Spreading some cushions on the floor, I set up a bed for him next to mine, so he would sleep for a while, and tried to calm him down by telling him that later in the morning, after it cleared a bit, we would return to Galilea, help the people there, and take Harry with us to heal the angel.

"He's not sick, he is possessed by Mermeoth," he explained.

Although exhausted, Orlando was so overwrought he couldn't sleep. He tossed and turned like a convict in his death cell, kicking off his blanket and upsetting the cushions. Meanwhile, I was trying to finish the tape transcriptions, which had to be delivered in a few hours, so I turned on the television and let him watch a cable TV movie, which immediately entranced him.

While Orlando was watching a woman take off her heels in order to flee from a pack of Dobermans who wanted to eat her up, I reached out from my bed, started to pat his head, and asked, "Orlando, you are Ara's son, aren't you?"

"Yes."

"And the angel's brother?"

"Only on my mother's side."

"Why haven't you told me?"

"Crucifija said that was for strategy. When I became a

guide for newspeople, we all agreed not to tell anybody. So the people didn't think it was for publicity, and so they believed I was impartial about this angel thing."

"Tell me the truth, Orlando. Do you really believe your brother is an angel?"

"I know he is an angel."

"But tell me, how can you be so sure, I mean, he doesn't even have wings . . ."

"He doesn't have wings because here on earth he is disguised as a man."

I did not ask the boy who his father was. The graffiti on the wall had already told me.

The first horse is choleric red, the master of wars. The second one is melancholy black, the master of night. The fourth is the white mare of death. I, Mermeoth, am the pale third horse, faded by the winter sun. I am the master of storms.

I am Mermeoth, a horse's body with an albino angel's head, a centaur dissolved in the skies' reflecting waters. I am the ocean, I am every drop of rain and every tear. With my hooves I crack lakes as if they were mirrors. My nourishment is snow, and my teeth crush the crystals of frost.

My steps are not heard in the wet night. I am the horse and I am the horseman, solitary travelers across the opaline space. Lost in the mist, I seek the depth of a quiet, frozen pool. Pale horse, deep in the water, lost in dreams, dissolved in the foaming spray.

I am Mermeoth, and my veins are rivers. My gentle trot sinks into the vaporous and milky edges of the Way. The steam from my nostrils clouds over the windows of time.

I am the pale horse, crowned by the moon. I am her son, made from her moisture, from her serene iciness, from the gossamer web of her light. She crowns me with her soothing beams, her clear reflections calm my ragged nerves. She calms my madness, and then I am the gentle angel of the slow canter.

The moon lags behind. Bad omen. The wind ceases.

Well do I know the calm before the explosion. I discover the smell of destruction in the air. I feel the tightness trying to get hold of me. I know I am on the verge of crossing the threshold.

Before me, the domain of aura. Infinite expanse, metallic, solid, electric, bright to the point of cruelty, without a trace of shadow to fend off the light. No secluded corner where I can seek refuge.

An unhealthy vapor rises from my limbs and permeates my mind. These plains, luminous and without shadows, portend sorrow, and in them the seeds of madness thrive.

I want to turn back, but I fail. My gallop becomes capricious and irregular. My flanks are lathered with the froth of my anguish. A horrible lucidity invades my mind. It is the aura, I know it, I have gone through it before. I cannot bear my own thoughts, thoughts that shoot through my head like darts, fast and piercing. Every memory becomes clear, every idea unbearably precise. I know what is coming, and I shudder.

I want to shield myself, I cannot stand the excesses of my own thinking. I must turn off this lacerating clarity, get rid of it, like the hand that drops the burning block of ice.

I want to hide from this light, but it comes from my own

memories. *The terrible light that banishes all shadows comes from within. I flee from myself, my gallop turns frantic, crazed, possessed. I step on faces, arms, and legs; I crush whatever falls under my hooves. I swamp the world with heavy slime, I flood space with my sweat, I demolish mountains and towns, I slaughter multitudes on my way.*

But there is no hiding, no escape. I feel the bolt coming, and I stop short, thwarted, helpless. I am motionless, and I wait. The back of my neck foretells the sharpness of the ax, a thick fear dilates my flesh. My tense muscles are about to burst, each of my sinews is stretched to the point of delirium.

And when the bolt strikes, it is definitive.

Its discharge blasts me. Its hatred makes me rear, tempered like a bow, crucified against the sky. I am a living conflagration, I vomit lava and spit stars as I disintegrate.

When the bolt dies out, it lets me fall. Broken puppet with demolished bones, charred brain. Incinerated from within. Only archangel ashes remain of me, blown away in the wind.

The bloodless dark debris on the ground is me. Mermeoth the Angel, Great Lord of the Waters, drowned in a puddle of his own urine.

Whatever happened to my angel? Between him and me stretched the endless morning, the unbearable traffic, the pitifully flirtatious blustering of my editor in chief, who took forever to read my article before he let me go, and Orlando's torpor: When I got back to my apartment, he was still asleep on the carpet. Although I was choking with anxiety, it was not till two in the afternoon that Orlando and I were able to get back to Galilea. Harry Puentes did not come with us; he had work to do.

Contrary to what everybody expected, it was a bright day on the mountain, as if nature had cleansed itself of its poisons during the night, and the sky, with its innocent shade of blue, seemed to be saying, "Don't blame me." Where was the catastrophe? There was no evidence any-where. On the contrary, the rain seemed to have scrubbed the neighborhood clean, making it look as if it had just come out of the laundry.

As we walked by the church, we heard Father Benito's voice hollering warnings over the loudspeakers. The revolving door swallowed Orlando but spat him out again right away.

"Come, Monita, come into the church to see them."

"To see whom?"

"Come see them first, and then I'll tell you who they are."

"Not now, Orlando, I want to see what happened in your home."

"It has to be now."

It was useless to try to get away from Orlando while he was tugging at my sleeve, so I followed him. There were only a few people inside, and my attention was drawn to a group of five or six youths standing at the rear of the church, throwing their weight around, and wearing T-shirts flowing outside their blue jeans, brand-name sneakers, and scapulars on their necks, their wrists, and even their ankles. I asked Orlando who they were, and he said he would tell me outside.

Father Benito was rattling on about the incredible powers of angels, who, being so numerous on earth, become extremely dangerous when they are not angels of light, who wish us well, but angels of darkness. As we walked out, he was still at it with his enumerations, which included, among others, the following items I was able to take down in my little notebook: angels of average status have the capability to change the direction of the winds; cast shadows on the sun; stop rivers and cause floods; light up nights and prevent fires; create shortages and high prices; transport bodies from one place to another as was done to Elias, Abacué, and Saint Philip; grant the power of speech to animals that are by nature silent, like when the angel made Balaam's donkey talk; stretch from one place to another without touching anything in the middle; and penetrate the human body, plumbing the depths of heart and mind.

"Did you see them?" Orlando asked, once outside. "It's them, a third-rate little gang. They go around showing off, and mugging people with homemade clubs. That gang used to be called Stinky Feet."

"And what are they called today?"

"Now they're the D.T.F.A."

"Like the ones who signed the graffiti."

"Right."

"What does D.T.F.A. mean?"

"I had a friend who was one of those Stinky Feet, but he is in jail now."

"A friend your age?"

"More or less, but, boy, did he get jinxed. He stole a TV set from a lady and had the bad luck of selling it to, of all people, one of her uncles, who bought it without knowing whose set it was, but when he realized it, he returned the TV to his niece and fingered my friend, and that's why he's in jail, see, but since my friend's friends weren't going to take this lying down, the woman's uncle had to leave the neighborhood, and anyway, in the end, the lady's TV set got stolen again by another gang called the Caps, because that's what they wear—baseball caps—and they cover their faces, but I don't know why, 'cause we all know who they are. Their leader acts as a policeman one day, and a thug the next . . ."

Orlando's stories were unraveling like streamers, each one attached to the tail of the one before, until we got to Barrio Bajo. What we saw left us dumbstruck.

In a clean sweep, without leaving behind any debris, the water had carried away four or five of the lower houses. The alley looked the same, plastic garlands and all; only a few houses were gone, like a few missing teeth. A few of those who were left homeless were sitting on bundles and other junk they had salvaged, and there they remained, silent and numb, as if waiting in line to buy tickets at a movie theater. Others were staying with neighbors whose houses had suffered less damage. Everything was slow and peaceful, as if life were proceeding as usual.

"Anyone killed or hurt?" I asked the first person we met.

"No, only property losses."

We saw the pink house above, apparently undamaged, and climbed up to it.

We were greeted at the door by Marujita de Peláez, who was sweeping out the mud with a broom.

"How good of you to come, but it's all over. He's sleeping now, like a saint."

"Did he have a seizure?" I asked her.

"One of the worst ever. The devil got into him through his little finger, went on to his wrist, then shook his arm like a rag, and finally threw him against the wall."

I immediately looked for the padlocked trunk with the journals. I had feared for its safety during the night, but there it was, undamaged by the deluge, like Noah's ark, its treasures intact.

The angel, life of my life, was lying on Doña Ara's cot, in shock, his body limp as if he had been trampled by the whole celestial marching army. But he looked more handsome than ever, a fallen god, but still a god. His body was so radiant that I feared the room would catch fire.

A small group of followers surrounded him, watching him with anticipation, perhaps wishing he would decide once and for all to rise, body and soul, to Heaven. Though I had entered on tiptoe and stood discreetly in a corner, it did not take long for his eyes, which had been waiting, to meet mine.

He looked at me and raised his hand. In a weak but sure and calm gesture, he reached out for me. I struggled through the crowd to get closer to his bedside, and inch by inch, my fingers reached toward his, and the moment we touched, I felt the universe shaking and new galaxies being born.

I knelt next to him and caressed his hair, still wet with perspiration, and in his pupils I saw faraway flashes of hallucination. The angel, still drowsy, just down from the cross, was mumbling those strange words of his, so harmonious and soothing, cryptic phrases that hypnotized me as I repeated them, and thus, holding his hands, I joined his trance as if nobody else existed. We journeyed through the crests of time, finally reaching a voice both familiar and adored, a voice that traveled twenty years back and returned to me in waves, like ancient blood familiar to my veins. There could be no mistake, it was the Flemish language of my grandfather, the Belgian from Antwerp, that now flowed from my angel's lips. I recognized it without understanding it, just as I never understood my grandfather when he rattled on in his native tongue.

I wanted that moment never to end, to endure the rest of my days, but suddenly, with what little consciousness still remained in me, I saw Crucifija repeat a gesture I'd seen her make before: using a small mirror she flashed light from a lightbulb intermittently on my angel's face. He came out of his languor to protect his eyes with his forearm, and when Crucifija tried to prevent him from doing so, Sweet Baby Killer jumped her and crushed her.

"What's going on?" I yelled.

"What's going on?" yelled everyone, startled.

"Don't let her! Don't let her!" Sweet Baby Killer cried out while practically smothering her victim.

"Don't let her what?"

"Don't let her do that to him with her mirror!"

"Do what with her mirror?"

Doña Ara came in, alarmed by the outcry, and spoke with an unfamiliar severity: "Everyone out! Only you two remain, and the family. And you too, Mona. Now tell me what this is all about."

The others filed out of the room, and when they had all left, Sweet Baby Killer tore the mirror out of María Crucifija's hands, and showed Ara what Crucifija had been doing with it.

"Look, Doña Ara," she explained, "with this mirror Crucifija brings on the angel's seizures. I realized this the other day."

Ara took the mirror and looked at it, bewildered, but I explained to her: "Those seizures your son has, Doña Ara, are surely epileptic seizures. Epilepsy is an illness, and it is terrible for those who suffer from it. What Sweet Baby is trying to tell you is that Sister Crucifija knows how to induce these seizures. That is, she knows what to do to provoke them. The flashes from the mirror trigger something in his brain, and he starts to have convulsions."

"But . . . I just don't understand. Why would Crucifija do something like that?" asked Doña Ara, fixing her intense gaze on the nun's empty stare.

"To get more people to come!" yelled Orlando, the only one who had not shouted yet. "She knows that the people like it better when he has a fit."

"Just a minute," Doña Ara said. "Sometimes he has seizures even when Sister Crucifija is not here."

"It's possible," I told her. "Sometimes these fits come by themselves. But when they don't, she brings them on. Sometimes it doesn't work, of course, and the people go home disappointed."

Stressing every syllable, like a judge pronouncing a verdict, Doña Ara spoke: "Sweet Baby, from now on you stay close to the boy, day and night, and if you see Crucifija doing harm to him with her mirror, or with anything else, you kill her. Did you hear me? You kill her. I hereby authorize you."

Then she turned to Crucifija: "And you, Sister Crucifija, you ought to know what's in store for you if you do this again. I warn you, death would be the least of your problems."

"Excuse me for saying this, Doña Ara," I interrupted, realizing this was my golden chance, "but your son has to be treated. I know where we could take him for treatment. It's not fair for him to suffer like this when there are medications . . ."

"All right, we'll take him to be treated," conceded Doña Ara. "But let me tell you one thing too, Mona, so there will be no misunderstandings. Whether the angel has epilepsy or whatever, that doesn't mean he's not an angel."

"That's clear to me. Get him ready, because I'm taking him with me. But before we go, Doña Ara, there are a couple of things you and I have to discuss in private."

We walked out to the yard. She sat down on the edge of the washbasin, the exact place where last Monday night I had met her son bathed in moonlight.

"Ara, we need to have an honest talk. Heart to heart."

"I have always told you the truth."

"Yes, but not all. Orlando is also your son?"

"He is."

"Yours and Father Benito's?"

"Miss Mona, try to understand."

"I understand, Doña Ara. I understand perfectly. But say yes or no."

"Yes."

"Please tell me about it."

She twisted the edge of her skirt in her hands and inspected the ground near her feet as if looking for lost coins. She began to talk, stopped after a couple of words, then started again. Suddenly she seemed to reach a decision, looked me squarely in the eye, and told me the whole story from beginning to end.

"Life wasn't easy. When the old priest died, my parents were already dead. I only knew how to dust saints and arrange flower vases for the altar. The church was my refuge, the only place where I felt comfortable. As long as the old priest lived, I used to spend hours talking with him, or listening to him play hymns on the organ. He taught me, may he rest in peace, how to write and everything else I know, and he lent me books on the lives of the saints, which I read one after another.

"In that church there wasn't a corner I was not familiar with, that wasn't mine. I liked to climb to the bell tower, feel the wind against my face, and look down on the city. I let my eyes search every street, every square, imagining that my son had to be out there somewhere, and that one day, from up there, I would spot him, and I would go running down and take him home with me.

"I also liked to stay in the basement, with its cold smell and its heaps of saints with broken noses. On sunny afternoons I used to sit on the altar steps with a tube of Brilliant and polish the paten, the goblet, the candelabra, until they shone so brightly they blinded me. I didn't even dislike the Christ, the big and bloody one who scares everybody. On the contrary, I felt he was my friend, and I would talk to him, tell him what I dared tell no one else, and ask him to help me find my son. Since he is way up there, I would climb high on a ladder to wash his wounds, making believe I could soothe his pain. Every so often, I would remove his hair, which is a wig of real hair, and shampoo it three times. Then I curled it, dried it with a hair dryer, and put it back in place, so he would look well groomed. The old priest would say, 'What do you think, Ara, that the Christ is your doll?'

"With the crown of thorns it was different. I would remove it and hide it, because I was thinking about how much it must be bothering him. I would keep it hidden until the old priest noticed its absence and started shouting, 'Ara, Araceli, Christ's crown has been stolen!' I then would bring it out of its hiding place and tell him that I was just cleaning it so it wouldn't get rusty.

"But as it happened, the old priest died and then Father Benito came and took charge of the parish, the church and everything in it, including me. But with Father Benito things weren't the same, because he imposed an additional duty on me, an unpleasant duty. You understand me, Miss Mona?"

"Yes, Doña Ara. And from that duty Orlando was born, right?"

"That is right. Then the town gossips started to talk, and

Father Benito got nervous and told me that if I wanted to keep my job, I had to get rid of the child. Can you imagine? He was making me hear those words again, the same words that had turned my life into pure suffering! The priest knew how to pressure me because the only thing I knew how to do was dust saints, and outside of the church the world was a mystery to me. But I had made up my mind. They would have to kill me before I would give up another baby of mine. So I left the church and went with my baby to whoever would take me in, trying to take care of him with what I could make washing clothes, which wasn't enough, and the truth is, we were practically starving.

"Father Benito wanted to see me utterly defeated so he could then reach out to me and impose his terms. But I did not budge; I would die before going back. We were having a hard time, Orlando and I. He was growing up and my mind was always elsewhere, thinking of my older son, the one I had lost. In those days Orlando was the one who took care of me. Even as a small child, he worried about me eating enough, whether I rested, and every afternoon he would go with me searching for his brother. He was so good to me that, after some time, it seemed like he was my mother, not the other way around.

"At this point I was already obsessed with my journals, totally involved in writing, and it was then that María Crucifija entered our lives. She read what I had written and became interested. She asked me to work with her, said that I had a good disposition."

"To work doing what, Doña Ara?"

"People were saying that she was a witch. Perhaps she was, I don't know. The fact is she made poultices and healing ointments, said prayers in homes to ward off evil spirits, and performed exorcisms on people besieged by bad luck. Crucifija earned her pennies, and as I was her assistant, this became the source of income for the three of us. Some time later, a lawsuit that had entangled my father's will was settled, and they gave me this house, so we moved in. After that, thank God, the angel appeared, and you already know the rest of the story."

"I see. But you and Crucifija don't see eye to eye, right, Doña Ara?"

"It depends on how you look at it, Miss Mona. True, she has her zeal for power, which at times makes her a bad person. But it also sharpens her wits. Consider all the good things that have come my way since we got together: first some income to live on, then the success with the lawsuit that provided a roof over my head, and finally the reward for my long search, the miraculous appearance of my son. Yes, there are problems with her, you have seen them, and it's necessary to keep her under control, but you must also consider that my two sons and I live off the alms, the offerings, and the donations she manages to collect."

"Excuse me for being so brutally honest with you, Doña Ara, but just as you told me the truth, I must tell it to you. Don't you think that this lady is using your son, I mean, that she is exploiting the angel cult? This can be very harmful to your son, don't you think?"

"To some extent perhaps, but, on the other hand, consider and you'll see, Miss Mona, that thanks to Crucifija my son is respected by the people of Galilea. Respected and admired and, I could even say, adored. What would have become of him if Crucifija had not realized he is an angel?"

I had no answer to Doña Ara's impeccable logic. But there was something else bothering me, and the moment had come to take it up with her.

"One last thing, Doña Ara. What about this gang calling itself D.T.F.A.? I noticed they have scrawled some offensive graffiti on the walls, and I would like to know what it is they have against you. Do you know what the letters *d-t-f-a* mean?"

"Yes, yes I do. They mean 'Death to the False Angel.' "

"That's what I was afraid of. Do you think they might want to kill him?"

"Well, up until now they haven't killed anybody, as far as we know. They do rob and assault people, yes, and they rape girls. But kill, no, they haven't killed, although lately people say they're getting awfully brazen, led on by Father Benito, who blamed my son for the deluge and the loss of the houses. Perhaps he has a point there, because as soon as my son started to buck up, the houses began to slide down. Father Benito said the proof it was his fault is that the punishment fell on Barrio Bajo, where the most heretical live."

"And doesn't Father Benito also say it's precisely in Barrio Bajo that the houses are the flimsiest and the land the steepest?" I fumed.

"That kind of reasoning won't convince anyone around here."

"What you're saying is very serious, Doña Ara. You

think that those D.T.F.A. boys are following Father Benito's orders?"

"No, not really. They're acting on their own. What I do
think is that Father Benito's rage, which spews on them from
the pulpit, gets into their souls."

She left it up to me to take care of the angel's medical
treatment, and started preparing him some cornmeal with
cinnamon in case he felt like eating.

The threat was reason enough to act at once, so I decided
to get going, and quickly. The first thing I needed was a
telephone.

The Vengeance
of Izrafel

FROM THE PHONE IN THE BAKERY I CALLED OFELIA MONDRAGÓN, a very dear friend and old classmate with a doctorate in psychology. She devoted her morning office hours to helping rich kids stay away from drugs and get closer to their parents; in the afternoons she worked as a volunteer in a women's public hospital for the mentally ill, commonly known as the Madwomen's Asylum. The poorest, most violent and forsaken of the city's disturbed women landed there, and amid the squalor and the plundering of hospital equipment, they were taken care of by people with the selflessness of saints. If they could not be cured, at least they were given some comfort.

The hospital telephone kept ringing and ringing, and I was boiling with impatience, until someone felt charitable enough to answer and tell me I would be put through. Minutes ticked by, and all I heard on the other end were distorted echoes, which sounded like muffled screams, as the phone kept swallowing coin after coin.

I felt uneasy connected to the dark world of the insane, as if it harbored some contagious virus that could travel by wire and penetrate my brain through my ear. Perhaps my persistent irrational fear of dementia comes from the belief that sooner or later it will be waiting for me just around the corner—that I'll only have a few more blocks to go before I knock on its door and enter, never to emerge again, just as my grandmother and maternal aunts had done. And also my mother, who, toward the end of her days and because of this hereditary curse, fell victim to a full-blown arteriosclerosis that filled her bed and her imagination with little green dwarfs, jumpy and meddlesome like an army of frogs.

No one was picking up the receiver at the other end. What if one of the crazy women had answered the phone and then forgotten my request? And what if Ofelia never came, and there was no one to save my angel from the bubble that surrounded and isolated him? And what if Ofelia did come and cured my angel, stripping him of his power and his magic? I was debating whether to hang up or keep waiting, when I finally heard her voice.

"Ofelia, I am with someone who needs your help. It's an emergency," I said.

"Can you bring her? I'll wait for you here."

"Right now?"

"Right now."

Everybody called my friend Lovely Ofelia. Her forehead, skin, nose, mouth, her oval face, were all reminiscent of the classical features on an antique medallion, but her eyes, enormous and often given to tears, seemed copied from Japanese comic books. Despite her degree from the Pontifical Xavieran University, earned by a thesis on the influence of the moon on depressive states, Ofelia trusted her intuition, which was so acute that it enabled her to perform unusual feats. Once, while we were with other friends vacationing at a beach resort, she lost a ring in the ocean and, before my eyes, recovered it in just a few seconds.

Freud had been unable to dissuade her from her conviction that chance, the unknown, and the supernatural play a decisive part in life. This belief caused her to invest part of her salary in lottery tickets, to make important decisions on the advice of the *I Ching* and the tarot, and to pay attention to the signs of nature—especially the appearance of certain birds, which could be good or bad omens—and, after breakfast, to interpret the pattern of the coffee sediments in her cup.

I had no doubt that Lovely Ofelia was the best person to appeal to in my outlandish and urgent predicament.

A crew of twelve women, which did not include Crucifija, was organized to transfer the angel to the hospital. Thirteen people in all, including Orlando tagging along. He was very distressed because the night before, when he had rushed to my house without telling anybody, he had given Ara a big scare, was scolded for it, and then topped that transgression with another one that morning by cutting school.

I wanted to leave right away, for I had a premonition that getting to the asylum was not going to be easy. Ara might change her mind, Crucifija could interfere, or the angel might have another fit, making it impossible to move him. Just to carry him was going to be a feat of epic proportions that we could have avoided if we had Harry's Mitsubishi.

There seemed to be no way we could get moving. Something kept coming up: we had to wait for Marujita de Peláez to feed her pets; it would be better to give the angel water before we left; so-and-so had to change her shoes; someone else had to go borrow money and would be right back. My angel, in his regal, almost archaic serenity, observed our comings and goings as if we were hysterical ants, and his beautiful face showed his perplexity, like someone trying to make sense of a soccer game in which both teams are wearing identical uniforms.

Finally we got the expedition under way, the angel hidden under a canvas tarp on a stretcher carried by four women. We had not advanced fifty steps when, as I had feared, we encountered an obstacle. It wasn't Ara's change of mind or Crucifija's opposition, nor did the angel have another fit. It was Father Benito, who was approaching armed with a crucifix, a bottle of holy water, and the foul smell of thirty cigarettes a day emanating from his mouth and nostrils, his grimy glasses and singed eyebrows. Decidedly on the warpath, he was followed by an altar boy and three of the D.T.F.A. boys I had seen in church.

"Stop!" the priest yelled, blocking our way and brandishing the crucifix. "Where do you think you are going?"

"None of your business, Father," Ara replied.

"Yes it is! By your heresies you are unleashing God's wrath on this neighborhood. And you tell me it's not my business?

Haven't you done enough harm with the deluge and the destruction of those homes? How many more disasters do you want to cause?"

Father Benito was addressing only Ara, reproaching her dramatically. Despite its bitterness, their encounter betrayed the unmistakable familiarity of two people who at one time had shared the same bed.

"Let us through, Father," Ara implored, her voice too meek for my taste.

"The boy isn't leaving this place without an exorcism," Father Benito declared, now addressing the whole group: "Back, back to your homes! He's got a demon in him, and we are going to get that demon out!"

I could not stand any more of this unbearable mix of ignorance, arrogance, and nicotine breath. Images crossed my mind like evil shadows: the obscene figure of the priest raping Ara in some corner of the church, persecuting her sons to get them out of the way, then sowing hatred against them from his pulpit. I was overcome by disgust and indignation, and started yelling at him—didn't he understand we were not dealing with a possessed person, but with a sick boy? I warned him that nothing would stop us, and called him a troglodyte and some other things I can't remember. I was barely halfway through my tirade when the surprised stares of everybody around me made me realize that none of this was any of my business. I had not been assigned any speaking part in this script and no one welcomed my participation.

Father Benito only had eyes for Ara, and reprimanded her in a fatherly way, asking her not to continue causing any more problems, and reminding her that he was there to help her. He even begged her not to be stubborn, not to insist on proceeding further.

What was going on? Why was I so naive? Why is it so hard for me to understand what motivates people? This was not a priest demanding obedience from a parishioner, nor a man angry at the woman who had left him. This was a man in love begging for some attention.

"Step aside, Father," Ara said again, "or I'll go straight to the bishop and tell him a thing or two about you."

There was no real anger in her voice either; just annoyance, or rather resentment mixed perhaps with a bit of flirtation. But it did not matter. Those of us who were carrying the angel felt her threat had gained us ground, and that we could move ahead.

"No, Ara, you can't do this," the priest exclaimed in a forceful tone, and we, the angel people, backed up a step.

"Yes, Father, I can and I will." We stepped forward again.

"All I'm asking is that you let me exorcise him. If he's got the demon in him, we'll get it out and we'll all be happier, starting with the boy." Benito was now conciliatory, and we, the stretcher people, stayed put.

"Over my dead body would I place a son of mine in your hands, Father, because there is only one demon around here, and it's you." Now we took several triumphant steps forward.

The priest had moved close to Ara and was now almost talking into her ear.

"Not a demon, Ara, just a man. A man destroyed by loneliness." I, too, had stepped closer in order not to miss a word. "And it's your fault, Ara, because you did not want to do things as God intended them . . ."

"Don't you lie using His name . . ."

What was taking place, beneath the religious conflict, was a lover's quarrel, plain and simple, a struggle between the two halves of a broken couple, with one of them zealously striving for harmony, using authority where persuasion had failed.

The three D.T.F.A. thugs threatened to take possession of the stretcher and make off with the angel, but Sweet Baby Killer paralyzed them with a roar that made it clear she was ready to break their necks.

"You stay out of this, lady!" the priest shouted at Sweet Baby Killer.

"Yes, Sweet Baby. Don't worry, I'll take care of this," Ara agreed.

"Not by force, boys. We will not use violence." It was now Father Benito's turn to calm his troops.

The antagonists, uncomfortable in the presence of others, showed signs that they would have preferred to continue the quarrel in private.

"Send your boy home, Ara, and come to the church for confession. There are ways to settle things."

"No. I have nothing to confess, and there is nothing to settle either."

"Don't say later that I didn't reach out to you."

"Let me go through, Father. I'm taking my boy to the hospital."

"I'm not moving an inch."

"I'll tell the bishop . . ."

The priest grabbed her wrist while, behind the eye-glasses, his impatience was finally shining through his myopic, beady eyes.

"Don't threaten me, Ara. Go tell the bishop anything you want. He won't believe you. Besides, I was within my rights to enjoy the services of a Tridentine maid. The church allows it."

"That's what you call it, Father? A Tridentine maid?" With a jerk, Ara pulled her arm free.

"You are going too far; you'll be sorry, Ara. Do you hear me?"

"Move away, Father," Ara insisted, her voice trembling.

"I won't say another word because there are too many people here. But this is not the end of it, Ara. No, Araceli, believe me, it is not."

The priest stepped aside and motioned his gang to do the same. We walked past them, heads high and contemptuous, bearing our undefeated angel on his stretcher. We proceeded downhill over the first section of the road, the most slippery part, as far as the bus stop. Sweet Baby Killer then carried him on her back, with total devotion, grateful at each step for the honor and privilege.

"It wasn't so bad after all, was it, Doña Ara?" I could not keep myself from asking.

"What wasn't so bad, Miss Mona?"

"Your living together with Father Benito."

She thought about it for a while.

"No, not really. I might have stayed with him if it had not been for my boys."

The angel sat by himself on the bus, apparently enjoying the view from the window. For the final leg of the journey, from the bus stop to the asylum, some fifteen blocks through neighborhoods full of petty thieves and vagrants, we took turns at the stretcher. Needless to say, it was a huge effort: my angel seemed to be made of ethereal matter, but weighed more than a pile of rocks.

The Madwomen's Asylum, which no longer exists, was a popular local attraction. For years, people with nothing better to do on a Sunday would stroll there just to watch the crazy women, the way others go to the zoo to see the camels. This lack of respect for the inmates caused the director to have the famous inscription chiseled in stone over the entrance gate: "These are the premises of the mentally ill. We ask that you behave as reasonably as they do."

Later, the Sunday walks and visits without prior authorization were prohibited, but the inscription remained, and we, the Galilea crew, walked under it with our angel hidden under the tarp. Doña Ara showed no sign of hesitation, while I was riddled with doubt. I was arbitrarily guiding the angel's destiny along my own path and leading him away from his own, and I was afraid of the consequences. Perhaps my eagerness to organize everything according to my rational thinking was in fact the needle poised to burst the great bubble of many people's illusion, maybe the only one they would ever have.

I stopped a moment to ask Orlando his opinion, which I had come to trust.

"Do you think we're doing the right thing bringing him here?"

"I don't know."

"What do you mean you don't know? It would be the first time you don't know something."

"I don't know," Orlando repeated. Once removed from Galilea, he no longer had a clear grasp of the situation.

We reached a hallway with floor tiles—those small six-sided tiles, mostly white with occasional dark ones to form a flower pattern, so common during my childhood but rarely seen nowadays. The patios in my grandmother's house had these tiles, my maternal grandmother, the one who, as I already mentioned, ended up insane. Was there a connection? Were little hexagonal flowers, repeated ad infinitum, a key to insanity?

We asked an assistant for Dr. Mondragón, and she pointed to a deacon's bench where we could wait. We sat in a tight row on the bench, our hands on our knees, like orphans waiting for their First Communion. We waited for a long time.

The angel was sleeping, I was overcome by bittersweet memories, and Orlando was engaged in the useless endeavor of trying to sharpen one end of the stretcher pole with his pocketknife.

We stared inanely as a woman awkwardly cleaned the floor with a bucket of soapy water and a rag. The social worker explained: "She's one of our patients. When they exhibit good behavior, we put them to work so that they keep busy.

We kept on waiting. My angel had woken up and was smiling trustingly, still wrapped in the fog of his semiconsciousness. He did not know that I, like Judas, was about to hand him over.

"It's for his own good," I kept repeating to myself, "for his own good, and for mine, too."

Although I never had much trust in medicine, and even less in psychoanalysis, deep in my soul I was convinced that this time a miracle would occur, that a curtain would open in the angel's disturbed mind, and that his brilliant intelligence would shine through. At the same time, it terrified me to see the workings of my little mind, so middle-class: I wanted my love to become a common man, rather than continue to be a splendid angel.

Sitting behind her desk, the social worker was writing something in an appointment book when she was jolted by Orlando's shouts: "Look! Miss! The well-behaved lady is drinking water from the bucket!"

It was true. The social worker raced up to the woman and scolded her, sounding less convincing than a mother trying to persuade her son to eat his vegetables. "Imelda, dear, you know you mustn't drink that dirty water. Remember last time it wasn't good for you, and how sick you became? Give me the bucket, Imelda . . ."

Imelda was unhappy about having her libation interrupted and lunged at the social worker. She would have gouged her eyes out, or worse, if Sweet Baby Killer had not held her until a couple of attendants came and took her away. The poor social worker was quite shaken, and so were we.

We were still recovering when Lovely Ofelia appeared at the end of the corridor, her hair tousled, her white doctor's coat stained with some yellow medication, and a pair of showy, aristocratic amethysts, inherited from her great-grandmother, decorating her earlobes.

"Things get rather hectic here" was her apology for making us wait, while she brushed the coat with her hands and tried to rearrange her hair.

"Where is she?" she asked, after giving me a hug.

I pointed to the tarp, which we had closed during the bucket incident so the angel wouldn't get frightened. Ofelia lifted the canvas. There, with his torso propped up on his elbow, like an Etruscan king on his litter, my dusky lover was revealed in all his splendor.

Lovely Ofelia observed him in silence for a moment, and then sighed, "Who is this divine creature?"

Then, looking at me, she said in a tentative voice, as if not knowing whether she was dreaming, "He looks like an angel . . ."

"Well . . . that's what he is, an angel."

"Is he dangerous?" she asked me in a low voice so the others would not hear.

"I don't think so. He only unleashes the forces of nature—"

"Where did you find him?"

"In the Galilea district. I am writing an article about him." I tried to sound impersonal.

"Hello," Ofelia said to the angel, but he looked perplexed and did not answer her.

"He doesn't talk," I explained.

"And he doesn't walk either? Why did you bring him on a stretcher?"

"Yes, he does walk. But I think he just had an epileptic seizure; he's exhausted. Look, Ofelia, this lady, Doña Ara, is his mother, this is his brother, Orlando, and these are people from the neighborhood who accompany him and take care of him . . ."

"Pleased to meet you, hello, how do you do," she greeted them all. "What do you want us to do?"

"We want you to tell us what is wrong with him."

"We would have to keep him here for a few days."

"We are ready to leave him in your care," I quickly replied, without knowing what Doña Ara would say.

"The problem is," Ofelia said, "this is not a hospital for men."

"Well, don't they say that angels are sexless?"

It wasn't difficult to convince her to ignore regulations and take care of my angel. The tarp was closed again, and the two attendants from before carried the stretcher into the depths of the hospital. Joining the cortege, we all walked from tiled flower to flower through that world, so familiar to me and at the same time so feared, of those consumed by an anguish they can neither decipher nor share.

I remember with particular intensity crossing at some point a vegetable patch where I had the perfectly clear sensation of being in limbo. There were some green stalks, perhaps onions, growing in irregular patterns in five or six furrows of black soil, all surrounded by high walls. We were in a courtyard, a separate space with a piece of white sky. Inside that rectangle where time had stopped, a few women were roaming around. Their movements were slow and divested of purpose. They were holding plastic shovels in their hands and sticking them into the soil again and again with absolute resignation and infinite patience, unaware of the onions, and anything else for that matter.

Ofelia explained that these were patients prone to frequent fits of aggressiveness who generally arrived at the asylum in a frenzied state after being found in the street blindly hitting people with sticks. The police would drag them in by the hair and throw them at the door. It was necessary to keep them heavily sedated.

I always thought that insanity should have an intense odor, an unmistakable emanation, but I was wrong. The asylum, disconcertingly, did not smell of anything, not even filth. I walked as if I weren't touching the ground, through that slow and odorless world, while telling Ofelia all I knew of the angel's history, leaving out the part relating to me, and giving her my irresponsible layperson's psychological diagnosis.

"I think what he suffers from is epilepsy," I said, "and that he is in a sort of autistic or deeply uncommunicative state that stifles his supernatural intelligence. He speaks several languages, of that I am sure, and when you are with him, you get the impression that he understands things better than you do."

"Do you really think he is an angel?" she blurted out.

"If I say yes, will you commit me too?"

"I'm serious." Ofelia laughed.

"Judge for yourself."

She asked me to leave him with her for two weeks. He would be kept in isolation while they performed an electroencephalogram and other tests, and in the meantime she would personally observe him closely and ask other psychiatrists for their opinions.

"What do you want, that I leave him here with you, by himself?"

"It's best that way."

Doña Ara was against this and became very upset at the idea of being separated from him for the first time since their reunion. She finally agreed after Ofelia swore to God that she would give him special attention and that on Sunday, after four days, she would give him back, no matter what. Ara looked at me as if demanding that I confirm the agreement, and I took her hands, assuring her that everything would be all right.

We abandoned the angel in the heart of the labyrinth. The gates were closed, the corridors got longer, and at the exit we said good-bye. Ofelia requested that Doña Ara stay at the asylum for a little while longer so that they could have a talk. The rest of the people from Galilea went their way, and I went mine. Without the angel, we had nothing in common.

I remember, and my memories are anger. Whoever awakens my memories will unleash my vengeance.

If he relives the dark rivers he has traveled, this celestial youth who sleeps peacefully at your feet will become the Terrifying King, and from his throat bitterness will roar.

If the wings of the past touch me, my eyelids will lose their calm, my dreams their transparency, my soul its peace.

I must not re-create the riddle of what has been. Like a beast driven mad by the smell of blood, memories would burst my veins.

Let the white, heavy void cover like a sheet the canceled landscape of what has already been lived. Let every shadow, every outline, every chiaroscuro fade under the dazzling brilliance of intense noon.

Let me forget, for with forgetting comes blindness, and also forgiveness.

Let Izrafel the Terrible, the Avenging Angel, not awaken in me; let not hatred make him draw his sword.

Let not me, Izrafel, extend my punishing hand over the sinful city, because none of its citizens would survive, nor their children, nor their children's children, nor even their dogs.

Do not ignore the sharpness of my sword, because revenge is its sacred duty, and it has descended three times on the night of the human race. On the first night, it laid waste the city of Jerusalem, beheading sixty thousand men of the tribe of Israel, from Dan to Bersabée. On the second night, it fell on the sleeping encampment of the Assyrian king and killed one hundred and eighty-five thousand men, leaving their bodies exposed to the morning mists. On the third and last night, it decapitated the firstborn of all Egyptians. On the fourth night, witnessing the horror spreading over the universe, the Lord my God, commander in chief of the celestial armies, took pity on his sub-

jects, and in a weary voice, this He ordered: "Enough, Izrafel, Exterminating Angel, withdraw your hand, sheath your sword. Your Lord's anger has been satiated."

If on the fifth night I realized that the time had come for more punishment and drew my sword, who could withstand the new surge of great fury? All fire, hail, rock showers, rats, teeth of beasts, poisons from scorpions and serpents, conflagrations, leprosy sores, ropes of the hanged: all punishment would come down on earth, and I would deliver it.

I am Izrafel, and I have forgotten my purpose and my name: do not wish me to remember.

I would exact torrents of blood from the homicidal city for each offense received. I would be so brutal that the descendants of men would rather die. They would run after death, and death would flee from them.

I am Izrafel, I gather affronts and am full of pain. I was the one with the open wound, and the river waters turned red when I bathed in them. My sadness is greater than the heavens.

Do not awaken what is sleeping under my skin. Let me be blind and deaf and mute; let me be innocent, ignorant, naive. Otherwise I will be a murderer.

I am Izrafel, and I have lost my memories. Do not encourage me to find them, because the confusion of the past would overwhelm the peace of the present, and the city down there would be reduced to ashes.

Do not ring the bell that would awaken my senses, let the wounded beast within me remain in hibernation.

I feel I am in the remotest corner of heaven, withdrawn into myself, my soul obliterated, my eyes shut tight against the past. *I run from myself and from the story of my life, hiding within myself.*

I am Izrafel: Do not summon me, do not aggravate me, for you will find me implacable.

Thus, silent and far away, I am well. I find peace in the color white. Let me sleep. Let me float. I want only to sail the un-named waters of forgetfulness.

Searching for my angel's past, I thought I would find heaven and ended up in hell. The journey back in time started Thursday at dawn, while I was asleep. I was dreaming the most annoying of my recurrent dreams: I was having dinner at my mother's (dead many years ago in real life), and she placed before me many dishes and platters with no food on them. I tried to explain, without offending her, that I could not eat because there was nothing there, when the telephone rang, waking me up. It was Lovely Ofelia.

"Did something happen?" I asked, startled, still engrossed with my mother's empty platters.

"Everything is all right. Your angel had a quiet night, and this afternoon we're taking him to a medical center for tests. I am calling you to discuss something. A detail. It may be true or not, I don't know. You might be interested."

"Of course I'm interested. Go on."

"It's about a patient at the asylum. Her name is, or she calls herself, widow Matilde de Limón. I'd like you to have a talk with her. She assures me she has seen your angel before."

"It may have been in Galilea."

"That's the strange part. It wasn't there."

"Where was it, then?"

"I'd rather you hear it from her. Come to the asylum, and ask her to tell you herself."

"Are you suggesting I interview a madwoman?"

"She's suffering from paranoid schizophrenia."

"And if she makes up a wild story?"

"That may happen. But she might provide a clue. To know something of the young man's past could be very useful."

While I was talking with Ofelia, I was more than once at the point of asking her offhand whether, since I was going to be at the asylum anyway, I could visit the angel. But I bit my tongue, in the first place, or rather in the second place, because I was sure she would tell me I had better not, and in the first place, because I was deathly ashamed that she might suspect my motive was hopeless love, not charity or human solidarity, nor even professional interest.

An hour later I was on my way to the Madwomen's Asylum in Harry's jeep. He had lent it to me for a week while he was abroad in exchange for my watering his plants and giving birdseed to a not-very-songful canary he kept in his kitchen. And why was I going to tell my troubles to widow Matilde de Limón, the paranoid schizophrenic? Why not? After all, for the past seventy-two hours and more, I had been living in the realm of utter folly.

This time there was indeed a smell. Rancid urine and boiled lima beans combined with vitamin B, pervasive despite the deodorizer that attempted to do its job but did not prevail. Entering the asylum unnerved me even more than it had the day before, perhaps because now I knew that *he* was there—no longer my knight of the verdant mountainside but an inmate amid all this squalor.

I looked for Matilde in the yard reserved for chronic patients. It was a bizarre place, with clothes hanging out to dry, planters, chickens, and other reminders of everyday life, in which every woman acted out her own drama of insanity and, at the same time, contributed to the overall atmosphere of extreme tension.

I still can't erase from my memory the Felliniesque images of that scene: an old lady, her breasts hanging out, clutching a live mouse in her hand; an executive type, who told me she was the legal representative of citrus industries for Latin America; a slender woman wrapped in a blanket, who said she was Saint Tomasa Molasses of the Holy Infant of Prague. The social worker led me to Matilde, a woman between fifty and sixty, who was dressed up as if for Mardi Gras, with kerchiefs and colored rags tied to her waist, head, and neck. She seemed eager to talk.

"What a pretty jacket!" She liked the suede jacket I was wearing. "You should give it to me. I have one like it, but at home, not here. I don't live here, you know. I have a huge house in the country. Very elegant, not like this. I'm going home tomorrow and I will never come back here."

"How nice, I'm glad to hear it."

"Are you a doctor?"

"No I'm not, I just came to talk with you."

"That's what they all say, they want to talk with you, and

then they spy on you and try to keep you here for life." Her tone of voice began to sour.

"Before you came here, Matilde, did you live in your country house?"

"I did not come here, they brought me. Now I want to leave."

"But there are good people here who take care of you . . ."

"Don't you believe it, they're pretending. They don't let me keep my pigeon. I have a little dead pigeon; it died when all the walls over there came down, and they made me bury it, the bastards. Would you believe it? Bury it! That's why I want to leave."

"Don't you have friends here?" I tried to find a way to lead her to the subject I was interested in before the persecution mania completely took hold of her.

"Friends? How can I have friends here, when everybody's crazy?"

"I was told that yesterday you saw a young man you used to know."

"He's my boyfriend. You know, when I dress up like this, with all these jewels"—Matilde proudly displayed her rags—"the men fall in love with me. But that priest who comes here doesn't let me have a boyfriend, he strictly forbids it, he says it's a mortal sin. But he's jealous of me, because I am really feminine, and he is only effeminate. You should see how he touches the men's hands, oh yes, yes indeed! That's the truth, but I'll be punished if I say it."

"Do you remember the name of the boy you saw yesterday?"

"Don't you have a comb you could give me? That's the problem. Since they don't let me have a comb or a brush, I walk around like this, all disheveled, look how tangled my hair is. It's not fair to be treated like this."

I looked for the comb I always carry in my handbag and gave it to her. As much as I could, I tried to make her stick to the subject I had in mind, but we were flying farther and farther from it, while the expression on her face was growing more and more bitter and desperate. Finally, widow Matilde de Limón dissolved into tears, and I did not know how to comfort her: whatever I said made matters worse. Fortunately, one of the interns from the National University came to my rescue, gently took away my comb, which she was twisting agonizingly in her hands, and told me it was better to end my visit for the day. To my great relief, he took her away.

The other social worker, the one at the front desk, let me use her phone to call Ofelia at her doctor's office.

"Doña Matilde de Limón didn't want to tell me anything," I reported.

"She didn't talk about the angel?"

"Not a whisper."

"Yesterday she didn't talk about anything else. If you can spare an hour, let's have lunch."

We agreed to meet north of the city at Oma's, at one-thirty. I zoomed off to *Somos*.

The triglyceride diet, fashionable in those days, was the subject foisted on me for my next article. It consisted of eating only proteins, no sugars or starches. For the piece my boss wanted, I was to interview Ray Martínez, leading man of the miniseries *Stormy Nights,* who claimed to have lost thirty pounds on the diet. It was ten-thirty, so I had time to take care of my ex-fatso before my appointment with Ofelia.

Ray Martínez, wrapped only in a towel, received me next to his bubble bath, while a masseuse administered a Japanese rubdown to his shoulder blades. It was hard to believe that this gentleman had achieved such an athletic physique by stuffing himself with fatty meats: barbecued ribs, bacon, and fast foods. Into my recorder he expounded a full tape on the philosophy of nutrition, Zen Buddhism, and weight, while I let my mind wander, trying to guess what Matilde de Limón might know about my angel.

Ofelia and I arrived at Oma's at the same time. The place was packed and we had to wait for a table. The music was so loud we had to shout at each other.

"I'm going to eat these chunks of butter," I threatened, impaling them on my fork.

"What are you doing!"

"Do you know who I met today? Ray Martínez. He lost weight eating fat."

"The triglyceride diet. They say it works."

"My mother's is even better: eating from empty plates."

"You had that nightmare again?"

"Last night. Do you think it means anything? That I didn't get enough motherly love, or something like that?"

"It's more likely that you went to bed hungry."

We ordered two steaming onion soups, and while we struggled with the melted cheese, which stretched to unmanageable strands, Ofelia decided to come to the point.

"In the phreno ward at La Picota jail. That's where Matilde claims to have met your angel."

"What's a phreno ward?" I asked, feeling needles inside and trying to pretend the subject moved me, but not too much.

"A jail for the criminally insane. The one at La Picota is a terrifying place."

"Tell me exactly what Matilde told you, and how reliable she is."

"As I told you, she is rational at times, and from what she has been telling us, we know part of her life story. It seems that her husband did time in that jail for the criminally insane, and might well still be there."

"Mr. Limón."

"Yes. Matilde visited him every week for years, until she cracked up too. As soon as she saw your angel, she started shouting that she knew him, that the youth had been her husband's yardmate."

"Did she mention his name?"

"The Mute. She said they called him The Mute."

Ofelia left, and I called a friendly secretary at *Somos* and asked her to get me two things for the following day: an appointment with an expert nutritionist famous for criticizing the diet based on fats, and a permit to visit the jail for the criminally insane at La Picota.

Taking advantage of having Harry's jeep, I took off for Galilea. Orlando had to be back from school by now.

"Orlando," I begged him while I invited him for a soft drink and bought him some soft sour sweets at La Estrella.

"Tell me everything you know about your brother. We have to put together the puzzle of his life. Do you understand?"

"It's all there, in my mother's journals."

"I want to know other things. For instance, where was he as a child?"

"It's a mystery, like Christ's past, nobody knows."

"Try to understand. You are very smart. Don't you think it must be horrible not to have a past?"

"Oh, yes, really horrible. I saw a movie on TV about a guy with amnesia after an accident, and he didn't recognize his wife, or his little children, and then this man—"

"You can tell me the story some other time. Now, think. There must be someone who knows something. Who could help us?"

"And then this man started walking the streets like a madman, and his wife, thinking that—"

"Orlando . . ."

"Oh, all right. Let's see . . . let's see. Well, it would be the Muñís sisters."

"The Muñís sisters?"

"Of course! They know everything, see everything going on in this neighborhood. Don't you know that they are soothsayers?"

"For this they don't have to be soothsayers. All they need to be is gossips."

"Oh no, no way! Listen to her!" Orlando pursed his mouth, the Bogotá way, to express his annoyance at my lack of common sense. "Don't you see they also know what is going to happen tomorrow? And next year? Eh!"

"Oh, all right. Take me to the Muñís sisters, then."

"Got any dough, Mona?"

"Some, why?"

"So we can tell them you want to buy some marmalade, and then they won't get suspicious . . ."

The Muñís sisters, Chofa and Rufa, did not live in Barrio Bajo but in the classier section of Galilea, two blocks away from the church.

"Miss Chofa! Miss Rufa! Any marmalade for sale?" Orlando yelled, and slipped into their house.

I waited outside on the street, subjecting myself willingly to the dizziness of heights while enjoying the breathtaking wide-angle view of the city below, interrupted here and there by a few wisps of mist.

A succession of food smells wafted toward me, one after another like entrées on a menu, so distinct that I could tell what people were cooking for dinner in each house on the block. In the blue one at the corner, for instance, they were surely cooking plantains; in the one with the rosebush by the door, beef was being pan-fried; across the street, some kind of soup with cilantro was boiling.

A donkey loaded with firewood passed by, and another one carrying pig swill; then, a couple of boys, eyeing my suede jacket or maybe my body, I couldn't tell which. They complimented me, calling out *Mamacita linda,* and went on their way. Finally, Orlando reappeared and ushered me into the house.

The Muñís sisters, surrounded by huge copper pots on a

coal stove, were immersed in the massive production of lemon-rind halves in syrup. They had quite an operation set up in their kitchen, with pots boiling and aromatic vapors filling the air, stacked crates of fresh fruit, used jars from which the original labels still had to be scraped off, sterilized jars ready to be filled, bins of sugar, and lots of knives, ladles, and strainers. The two Muñís sisters were bustling and fluttering about, removing a bitter taste here, adding a pinch of bicarbonate there, and then there were the rows of finished products: mamey marmalade, papaya preserves, guava jelly, canned tree tomatoes, and even coco plums in syrup. God, I hadn't seen coco plums since my grandmother, Mama Noa, served her grandchildren their share in bowls of fine English porcelain, five or six cotton-soft, bulging, pale purple plums. After we sucked all the pulp off the pits, war would break out along the corridors (those with the floor tiles I already mentioned) and up and down the stairs. If you were caught off guard, *pow!*, your head would get thwacked by a pit. Meanwhile, in her room, my grandmother was going through the torments of a severe arteriosclerosis that irrigated her brain with blood too thick to flow smoothly, making her burn with anxiety for our dead grandfather's return, and obsessed with brushing off all those irksome dead leaves falling endlessly on her bed.

The Muñís sisters became aware of my trancelike gaze at the sweet plums and asked if I wanted to sample them. Before I took the first one to my mouth, the clear memory of their particular half-faded sweetness came back to me, summing up my entire childhood.

The Muñís sisters turned out to be marvelous witches. Both wore aprons, like Mama Noa's, with large pockets, but while Rufa kept silent and listened, Chofa, whose hip was malformed at birth, jabbered away like a parrot. After the coco plums, they served us early figs, blackberries, and apricots, topped with a teaspoon of homemade caramel custard. They waited, arms akimbo, for Orlando and me to praise their delicious concoctions. I bought an assortment of everything to fill a box, and loaded it into Harry's jeep.

In the meantime, we kept the conversation going. To get Chofa to tell me all she knew of my beloved angel's history required only for me to ask. But first she wanted Orlando to leave, so she gave him some money and sent him on an errand to the store.

"It's better for the boy not to hear this," she told me after he, quite grudgingly, had left.

The first thing Chofa Muñís told me was that Doña Ara's father, Nicanor Jiménez, had been an alcoholic.

"He ordered people around but didn't do much himself; always full of booze, he was an unfeeling beast of the kind that thrives in this country. His solution to any problem was to unbuckle his belt and beat somebody up, anybody, starting with his wife. Her name, poor soul, was Lutrudis, and she wasn't bad, but she had the soul of a scared little rabbit."

"Nicanor Jiménez was the grandfather who gave the angel away to the gypsies?" I interjected.

"That is pure legend. Nobody gave him away to any gypsies. Whenever a baby got lost, people would say, 'The gypsies took it!' What he did was dump him with a mistress he kept in the La Merced area. That woman was no good and raised the kid without any affection; she hardly talked to him and barely fed him enough to keep him alive. But the baby kept growing and was very beautiful, very sweet, in spite of all this. He would sit and play in a corner with a jar, a stick; anything was good enough for him. He spent hours like that, without a peep; people said he never cried. Maybe, when his grandfather saw how beautiful the child was, he got the idea of making money off of him."

"Then he did sell him . . ."

"But not to the gypsies. I don't know where he heard about it, but there was a foreign couple, elderly and wealthy, who wanted to adopt a Colombian boy. He took his grandson, bought him some clothes, and brought him home to Grandma Lutrudis in order for her to get the boy ready, because he was filthy, shaggy, and malnourished."

"If the boy came back home, how come Ara didn't find out?"

"Don Nicanor arranged his coming to coincide with the week Ara spent on a yearly spiritual retreat that she never missed, at a convent in Boyacá. When she returned, the trail was cold; she never even knew her son had been there."

"Why didn't anybody tell her? And excuse me for asking, but Doña Chofa, and you too, Doña Rufa, if you both knew, how come you didn't tell this wretched woman, who was going crazy looking for her son?"

"In those days we lived very far from here," Rufa contributed for the first and last time. "We did not even know any of those people. What you are hearing are the stories my sister put together later from hearsay; we cannot personally attest to any of this."

"Pretty well planned, a neat job," Chofa continued, unruffled. "Nicanor took the boy to the foreign couple and asked for a high price. He knew he could blackmail them: they were not married, you see, they were brother and sister, and therefore could not make a legal adoption. They still must have haggled him down, though, and he had to lower his price further still since the boy did not speak. Everybody knew this because Don Nica was furious about it for a while and kept telling anybody who would listen how stingy those damn foreigners were."

"And Ara's mother, Doña Lutrudis, didn't she feel any compassion for her own daughter and grandson? I can't believe it."

"As I said, Lutrudis's only care was that her husband wouldn't belt her to death. But let's finish the story."

"Just a minute, Doña Chofa. Where were those people, those foreigners, from, do you know?"

"Somewhere in Europe, I don't know, it's a very big place. Once they had the boy, they left Colombia—which they hated—traveled a lot, and sent him to school; people say that the boy got to learn not one but several languages."

"So he was a happy child after all . . ."

"But not for long. The woman who adopted him, the one who really loved him, died in Europe, and her brother returned to Colombia, where they say he still had some business, bringing the boy along. He was already pretty tall by then. But the man had a vile temper and was much too old for the job of raising a boy. Besides, at eleven or twelve years old, the boy was already very muscular."

Just then Orlando came running back from his errand, not wanting to miss out on the story. Doña Rufa offered to double his tip if he would go to the market and bring her a bunch of curly parsley. Orlando thought it over for a moment and then accepted the deal, but on his own conditions: first, he wanted a glass of water, he was so thirsty, he said. Pausing at length after each gulp, he waited for Chofa to start talking, but she changed the subject and began giving me her secret formula for removing the bitterness from lemon rinds. The moment Orlando left, Chofa went on with her story.

"The boy had been shy and withdrawn, but when he became an adolescent, he got involved in the common problems of youth today. He tried drugs and became hooked on marijuana, maybe stealing from his adoptive father to support his addiction. That's the story a friend of mine told me; she was related to the mistress Don Nica kept at La Merced. The thing is that Don Nica, now cranky and decrepit, used to come to his lover's house and complain about foreigners not being trustworthy. It seems that after all those years, the man who had adopted the kid wanted his money back because the boy had turned into an addict. Don Nicanor, who was about as stingy as they come, didn't give him a penny, and his grandson landed in a drug-treatment center. And that is as much as I know. Then I lost the thread of his story."

"Until the boy reappeared, two years ago, on his mother's doorstep."

"Well, let's say that *a* boy appeared two years ago at Doña Ara's. Nobody knows whether he really is her son."

I waited for Orlando to return and hugged the Muñís sisters, who presented me with another couple of jars of canned fruit before letting me leave. Orlando and I got into the jeep without a word.

My angel's possible past history was taking shape before my eyes, piece by piece like a patchwork quilt held together with threads of pain.

"Now, tell me, Mona. He is my brother, and I have the right to know."

"Of course."

The most dreadful conversations often happen in cars, and this one was no exception. I told Orlando what I had heard in the gentlest way possible, carefully choosing my words, but as I spoke, a shadow of mistrust clouded his eyes. I wished with all my heart I had never attempted to find out the truth, so that I would not have to be the one to tell him now. But it was too late. Whenever I tried to leave something out, Orlando would notice, and that's how he led me on, all the way to the end.

"Better not tell my mother a word of this. Or anybody else."

He got out of the jeep without saying good-bye.

Thursday night I spent bouncing between insomnia and nightmares, hot as hell if I pulled up the covers and freezing if I pushed them off, dreaming of a child angel, abandoned and silent, playing alone in a corner. Friday morning I woke up determined not to visit the phreno ward for the criminally insane, and to stop investigating any further.

My intervention had reduced the celestial happenings of Galilea to common human misery. What sense did it make to subject the angel to therapies that would force him to remember, when his memories would be like shards of shattered glass piercing his heart, as well as his mother's, his brother's, even my own, and God knows how many others'? It was stupid of me to torch the angel myth, knowing that nothing would come from the ashes but cruel, human reality.

I was in no mood to get up when the telephone rang. It was Ofelia.

"I have good news for you. Yesterday we took an electroencephalogram and made a spinal tap. Your angel is indeed epileptic, but his symptoms can be controlled with a daily medication, and his seizures will probably not recur. That will make his existence more tolerable."

When I hung up, my soul had returned to my body, and I changed my mind again. What if no electroencephalogram or spinal tap had been taken? The seizures would have continued, day by day, each worse than the one before, progressively destroying him. You cannot, after all, repudiate the remedies human beings create to ease their ills. Doña Ara and Orlando would have to realize that although reality might present a horrible face, even worse was the distorted mask of unreality. The angel would need to undergo therapy to lift the veil clouding his vision. Only by facing his own past, no matter how cruel, could he recover his present and his future. I would indeed make a visit to the phreno ward and continue trying to unravel the truth.

I had been warned that the phreno ward at La Picota was one of the most infamous hellholes on earth, a living grave-yard, where human rejects were cast and left to rot.

"If you'll forgive me, miss, I don't think you want to go in-side," the guard at the gate warned me.

"Yes, yes, I do want to."

"Well, you can, of course. Your permit is in order, but I wouldn't advise it. At best, you'll pick up some of their lice."

"I want to go in anyway."

"You are not allowed in alone. You'll have to wait for a guard to go in with you."

"Do you remember a young man, some years ago—Think of the tallest inmate you ever saw here."

"I'm new here, and besides, I've already requested a transfer. This is no place for people. The stench penetrates everything, it's no use washing your clothes or scrubbing your body, the smell won't go away. This is no life, working here, no sir."

"Maybe there are files I could look at. Isn't there a regis-ter of the prisoners who have done time here?"

"Ask at the administration desk. They might have files."

"Don't you know the names of the inmates?"

"Don't you see that besides being criminals, they're crazy? Nobody calls them or talks to them, and they even forget their own names."

To pretend I wasn't there, I tried to close my eyes, ears, and mouth. I did my best to avoid touching the grimy gate or filthy wall, and I would have preferred not to step on the floor or breathe in the atmosphere overloaded with misery. Behind the iron bars, one could sense only dampness and darkness, and hear no identifiable voices, only coughs and muffled noises such as animals make when dying in their lairs. From the bottom of the pit came the smell of decomposition and hopelessness, and I felt a horrible urge to throw up. I was standing at the gates to the lowest possible level of existence, where human beings were reduced to refuse. I felt my strength leaving me.

A small one-eyed man appeared on my side of the gate, hosing down the walls and floors.

"Please step away, I'm spraying water and I don't want to get you wet," he warned, and although I did step away, he wet my shoes.

"You have a relative in here?" he asked.

"Fortunately not. Have you been working here long?"

"My whole life, so far."

"Then you could help me. Do you remember an extremely tall boy who was here some time ago?"

"As best I can remember, there were two or three very tall ones."

"He was dark-haired."

"They are all dark-haired."

"This one is hard to forget because he was extremely handsome. Try to remember . . ."

"No one is handsome in here. With the whole lot of 'em you couldn't make a stew."

"Think of him as a giant. I believe they called him 'The Mute.'"

"Most of them are mute. Mute and deaf and stupid. They howl and growl, but don't talk. That's what this place does to them."

"What a factory of angels" . . . I said under my breath, but the little man overheard me.

"Angels? Ha! That's a good one. A factory of angels! Did you hear that, González," he shouted to the guard. "She says this is a factory of angels!"

"Let's see what she says after going in there!" González replied.

"The boy I'm referring to was here for a few years, and then managed to get out," I insisted.

"Nobody gets out of here."

"This one did . . ."

"That would be a miracle. Of course, now and then when it gets too overcrowded, there's a cleanup and the worst off get thrown out."

I finally saw the guard coming to escort me in, and I panicked. "I can't do it, I can't do it, I can't do it," my heart shouted, about to burst.

"That's her," González said to the newcomer.

"Walk in," the new guy said, and taking out a bundle of keys, he started to unlock the gate.

"No! Excuse me, I can't. I've got to go. Where's the exit? Thanks, but no. I can't go in there."

Before I realized it, I was running. I don't know how I got my papers back, managed to find Harry's jeep, and locked myself in to fend off the horror. I drove without knowing what I was doing or where I was going. I was physically and mentally shaken, reproaching myself over and over with a maddening refrain: "So you're the one who says we must look reality right in the eye? But you can't! You coward, a thousand times coward, wanting to force a sick boy to remember all the years he spent in hell, when you can't even take it for a minute. So we have to face reality? Go ahead and try, you bullshitter. I dare you!"

I don't know when, but I arrived at the asylum. I had to see him or die. Lying to the nurses, I said that I had Dr. Mondragón's authorization. I did take a look at him, on a bed too small for his frame, more distant than ever, all wrapped in a cloud of his own. He had on a white gown with a number on the back, handwritten with a laundry marker, and it seemed now that his soul had really left his body, beyond recall.

"Why does he look like that, so sickly?" I asked the nurse.

"It's the spinal tap. It exhausts them and gives them a bad headache. You better make it a short visit so he can sleep."

I touched his hands and found them rough and dry, and also his feet, his perfect feet, which were cold and withered like dead animals. I asked the nurse for some body lotion, but she said there wasn't any.

I walked out to the only pharmacy in the neighborhood and asked for saline solution and a body moisturizing cream.

"This one is the best," the saleslady said, handing me a jar labeled "Doucement," and underneath that, "Contains Extract of Spikenard."

"Doucement? I never came across this brand before."

"Haven't you heard all the ads on the radio? By the way, you don't pronounce the *t.*"

"I see. May I open it?"

"Of course."

It was a thick, oily substance with a penetrating fragrance.

"The scent's too strong. Don't you have Nivea, or Pond's cold cream, or even Johnson's baby oil?" I inquired.

"Only this one. It's excellent—it's all the rage now."

I went back to his bedside and moistened his lips with the saline solution. He sat up a bit to take a couple of sips. He looked at me, and deep in his eyes I perceived a glimmer of recognition, but it faded at once. He sank back, and I began to apply the cream, very slowly, starting with his feet and the recent scar on his ankle, as if this were the starting point of the secret map of his body. All my love and all my determination went into this effort; I wanted to erase the scars of loneliness from his skin.

"Forgive us," I whispered, "for all you have had to suffer on this earth. Forgive, forgive us all the wrongs we have inflicted on you."

"How wonderful! Who brought in nard?" The head nurse charged into the ward like a gale. "This place smells of nard."

"It's this stuff." I showed her the cream.

"This boy is a beauty," she said, taking my angel's hand. "We are all in love with him here."

"I'm not surprised."

"But he doesn't take the bait." She laughed, and walked out again.

I left him asleep, and as I was leaving the asylum, I realized for the first time that no matter how much I tried to get close to him, we would always be light-years apart; no matter how much therapy or how many treatments he was given, he would always be a stranger on this planet.

On my way home, stuck in traffic jams, I got to thinking about Paulina Piedrahita, my semantics teacher in college. She said the word *nostalgia* was invented by Swiss mercenaries serving far away from their homeland, who were suddenly overcome by a desperate need to return home, which caused them great suffering. That is why, Paulina said, the word *nostalgia* comes from the Greek *nostos*, "return," and *algos*, "pain," and it refers to the moment when our thoughts return to some past place where we had been happier.

No matter what the doctors said, I knew that my angel's despondency was none other than his nostalgia for Heaven.

Lovely Ofelia and I had agreed to have dinner that evening at Salinas Restaurant, so we could talk at length about the angel. We were ready to blow a week's wages on a few dry martinis and some broiled crawfish. But the day had left me exhausted, with soul and stomach in turmoil, and a single crawfish might very well have triggered my final collapse. So I called Ofelia and asked her to come over to my place instead.

She arrived at eight sharp with a baguette and a thermos

full of chicken soup, assuring me it would do me good. Then she turned on the television; she could not miss *A Woman's Scent,* the soap opera broadcast at that time, and I had to wait for it to end before I could begin my questioning.

"Okay, now tell me what's wrong with him."

"Can't say. He's lost somewhere between mental retardation, autism, and schizophrenia. Very, but very, lost."

"But how can you say he's lost, when he can produce such writings? You have only read bits and pieces of the journals, but if you took the trouble to—"

"Just a minute, just a minute. We are getting tangled in some kind of warped logic here. To start with, the journals were not written by the angel; Ara wrote them. If you want to talk about the journals, let's talk about Ara. She really does fit the schizophrenic model, hearing voices and all.

"We'd better stop this conversation, we aren't getting anywhere. If you want to understand any of this, you have to forget your logic; it won't do us any good."

An uncomfortable and even hostile silence followed. After a prudent interval, Ofelia tried to soften the situation by asking me why I had taken this matter so much to heart.

"Well, it so happens that I am in love with this autistic, schizophrenic retard," I snapped at her.

"Very much like you. I should have known. Wait," and she sounded annoyed, "let me pour a splash of sherry into this broth."

We fell silent. Then Ofelia said, "Okay, let's start from the beginning. From that past you are trying to reconstruct."

I didn't want to go on. Suddenly the whole story seemed utterly absurd, and I felt ashamed and sorry for having told Ofelia the truth. Thank God I didn't mention that I had made love to him.

"Up to now," she went on, trying to break the ice, "you have only theories, and not all of them make sense. A cruel and alcoholic grandfather who gets rid of his grandson, a woman who raises him like an animal, an adoption that falls through because the boy gets hooked on drugs. Then a rehabilitation center, no doubt another nightmare, and after that, possibly a crime—we don't know which one—or an awful injustice, which lands him in jail. Since he is an epileptic and an addict, and is probably mentally ill already, he gets locked up in the phreno ward, where he really goes over the edge, but from which he manages to escape, God knows how. Then we take another leap of faith, and the boy, who has never been in his own home, never seen his mother, except when he was born, returns to her. To the locals he seems to have come down from heaven, and since he is also beautiful and strange, has seizures and speaks in tongues, they take him for an angel and make him the center of a cult. How am I doing so far?"

"Fine, except for one detail. The boy does know his mother's home. His grandfather took him there so that his grandmother could bathe him and get him dressed up, before delivering him to the foreign couple; although he spent only a few days there, it's perhaps the only place he has pleasant memories of, the only one where he has been well treated. So when he gets out of the phreno ward, he manages to return. It's plausible."

"Plausible, but not probable."

"Well, if this wasn't exactly his life, it couldn't have been much different."

"Do you know what usually happens to angels with such a past? When they finally face it, they are overcome by hatred. A kind of hatred, of despair, and a thirst for vengeance so enormous that, to control them, it would be necessary to wipe out their conscience. Therapy first changes such an angel into a demon. A sociopath. That would be the sign that he is on the road to recovery."

"Stop these warnings of impending doom. You sound like a regular Cassandra."

"Don't say that, not me. Well, let's forget it. Let's go on with our story. We got to the point in the life of the angel where you come along and fall in love with him, and bring him to the asylum so I can cure him. What's next?"

"You tell me. Do you believe anything can be done? Is there any possible treatment that will not turn him into a demon?"

"Well, to be honest with you, in his case treatment is not an option. We are talking about someone who doesn't speak, makes no contact with the outside world, does not look at anyone, and shows no affection for anyone. It's a hopeless case."

"No, Ofelia, not true!" I was as impassioned as a leftist at a protest demonstration. "It's not like that. You don't know him. You have no idea of the deep feelings he can convey.

Not only to me, but to thousands of people who travel to see him. Don't tell me, like my boss, that these are just poor people's superstitions. I'm telling you about something that isn't rational. He radiates light, Ofelia, and I am amazed that you, of all people, haven't noticed. He radiates an overwhelming love like no one I ever met. That's his way of making contact."

"Wait, wait, let's not wax poetical just yet. Let's stick to the facts. We don't know for sure who we are talking about, but let's assume it's a person who has lived under conditions of extreme physical and social deprivation that have caused irreversible damage. His epilepsy, untreated for so long, also contributed to his mental deterioration. I didn't want to tell you this, but we have on our hands a human being who does not even have the level of consciousness of an animal."

"That's precisely the point, Ofelia, perhaps we are not dealing with a human being. To Ara, to Orlando, to a whole community, he is an angel. The Angel of Galilea. Can't you see the difference?"

"No, I can't see it. I must confess I don't understand anything. Do you know what I'd really like? I'd like to know the truth about what this boy means to you."

I took my time thinking it over.

"For me, he represents the two loves, Ofelia, the human and the divine, which up to now have always come separately."

"And that's probably healthier, I mean, each one in its own place. Or if not healthier, at least more bearable, less overpowering. It worries me because I see you stuck in a terrible mess . . . I don't know, this is all so complex, and it really has nothing to do with psychology. Why don't you discuss it with a priest?"

"Not in this lifetime. There isn't a priest in the world who cares about what happens inside a woman's mind. They only want her not to sin with her body."

"But now and then you come across an intelligent, progressive one . . ."

"On that subject, they are all in limbo."

"Then why not try a priest who is an expert on angels?"

"Like who? Monsignor Oquendo, Archbishop of Bogotá? Do you know what archbishops do with angels who come down to earth to court women? They pluck their feathers and boil them in the stew pot, that's what they do."

"Let me see, how can I put this without offending you? Your angel seems to be altogether too much and, at the same time, too little."

"That's the way men are too, aren't they? What about your French intellectual, the one who was either on a plane or on the phone? Or Ramírez, the one I was madly in love with for two years, who was always so tired from work that I hardly saw him except when he was asleep? Or any of the others? Let's go down the list, and you'll see. What about the famous Juan-carl, who came to my house and said he loved me, and from there went to yours and gave you the same line? Let's see, who else? There's Enrique, a little boy with the pretensions of a world savior and, without going any further, your Santiago, such a good guy, who, because he is so wealthy and has so many employees, is convinced that whatever he does is earth-shattering. Any of these seem to you more consistent than my angel?"

"You make all of them sound bad, but that doesn't make your angel sound good," she replied, putting an end to the argument. "Let's not draw any conclusions yet. I'll keep him in observation for a few more days. Perhaps the change in environment and the separation from his people have made him more depressed than usual, and this keeps me from . . ."

Ofelia's inability to see the situation clearly stymied me. Aware of this, she didn't finish her sentence. Again we were silent.

"You know what I'm going to do?" I said at last, sounding just a bit vindictive. "I'm going to take him back to his neighborhood. Up there he is an angel, while down here he is nothing but a crazy idiot."

We had this talk on Friday night. By the following day, Ofelia understood.

I spent the morning at the gym, clearing my mind on the stationary bike and in the stupefying frenzy of aerobics. Then, around six in the afternoon, after finishing my piece on the new diet, I watched the news on television: a soccer fan had stabbed a corrupt referee to death, a district attorney had killed his two brothers-in-law because they were making noise with their motorcycles, a few guerrillas massacred some civilians whom they accused of being mercenaries, a few soldiers massacred some civilians whom they charged with aiding the guerrillas. In other words, routine stuff, the daily carousel of death to which we have grown accustomed. I was about to turn the TV off when Ofelia arrived, unannounced. I knew as soon as I opened the door that something had happened.

"You were right," she said as she walked in. "He is no ordinary person. You can't imagine what happened today."

She told me that he had met first with Father Juan, a Spanish priest from Asturias who for years has been coming to the asylum every Saturday to hear the inmates' confessions and to spend some time with them. Amazed by the angel, Father Juan had assured Ofelia that the young man spoke beautiful Latin and Greek. So Ofelia had asked Father Juan, "What did he say to you?"

"Yes, what did he say?" I also wanted to know.

"Father Juan, who is a pain, told me that he could not repeat what he had heard in confession. But he assured me it wasn't nonsense."

A while later, Ofelia continued, she noticed that an unusual silence had fallen over the asylum.

"What's going on in here?" she had asked one of the psychiatrists. "How come this place is so peaceful?"

But the psychiatrist had not noticed anything unusual, and Ofelia started to make her rounds, certain that there was something new in the air, until she got to the yard of the chronic patients.

"Your angel was in the center of the yard, and the patients surrounded him, with such placid expressions on their faces as I had never seen before, as if their souls were at peace. He dominated the space by his sheer size, and he looked so radiant that his veins seemed to be filaments of light. He moved among the patients gently, almost in slow motion, and without even looking at them, he gave everyone an affectionate pat on the head as if they really meant something to him. They crowded around him silently, with the serene attitude of people who feel at peace and are completely fulfilled. Actually this was all, only a particular state of mind that was imperceptible to the uninitiated—a group of medical students who were also there kept talking among themselves, totally unaware of what was going on. But for the inmates it was perfectly clear, though it was an almost imperceptible difference, the slightest turn of the screw, which had changed that nightmarish yard into a realm of love, bathed in a warm glow and enveloped in silent harmony. If you looked at the angel, you knew that all those good feelings were coming from him."

I poured a couple of double whiskeys, and we drank an emotional toast to our angel—not just mine, but ours. In contrast to last night, we were now on the same illogical wavelength, able to settle comfortably into a long, absurd conversation in hushed voices, so as not to awaken my aunt, who had gone to bed. We understood each other despite our elusive subject that defied all reason.

The drinks did their work and, surprisingly, rather than accenting Ofelia's scientific bent, they brought out the Samaritan side of her personality.

"Now I know we can help him," she said with the enthusiasm of a Florence Nightingale. "We must find a way to reach him, to establish contact. Who knows, maybe this angel is an envoy, sent to Colombia to end all the suffering and the killing, and maybe we can help him accomplish his mission.

Or maybe he's a prophet or a great leader. He'd even get my vote for president, since I like him better than any of those presidential pretenders. But, on the other hand, I frankly can't picture him as your husband."

"Well, he made love to me like a god."

"I can't believe it! Well, you would know. That's it! That may be the key, sexual therapy!"

"Maybe. Anything but your psychology. We've already proved it doesn't apply here."

"I agree, let's discard psychology, it won't work in this case, or in any other, for that matter. But we can try other things: spiritualism, hypnosis, fasting, meditation . . ."

"Only the hymn to the Holy Trinity works, believe me. You don't have to invent anything, all you have to do is repeat 'Holy, holy, holy. Holy is the Lord.' Don't you realize he is an angel, Ofelia? An angel, repeat with me, an *angel*."

"He might be an angel, but he still lives on this earth, in this city of Santafé de Bogotá, and he has to learn Spanish, and how to survive on his own, how to read . . ."

"Are you trying to tell me that someone who speaks fluent Latin and Greek has to be taught to read *'mi-ma-má-me-a-ma'*? Do we want to push him over to the other side? Please, Ofelia, let's not be so arrogant."

"Besides, he can't be your boyfriend," she argued, pulling one last persuasive gambit from her sleeve, "because he is at least twelve or thirteen years younger than you. He must be eighteen at the most, perhaps only seventeen."

"And who is to say he isn't four or five thousand years older than me? Who can calculate the age of an angel?"

"This is pointless," Ofelia sighed. It was already around ten, and we were saying good-bye at the door when she turned back in. I thought she had forgotten her coat or something, but she collapsed down again on the big armchair.

"What's wrong?" I asked.

"We didn't get to the worst part. Come, sit down, we might as well get it over with."

I prepared myself to listen as if opening my mouth at the dentist's to have a tooth pulled.

"I've told you this before, but let me remind you. The rehabilitation, if we do succeed with it—and this late at night I am inclined to believe we may—will change your angel into an ordinary human. All too human, do you understand? That innocent gaze of his will cloud over. You need to remember that."

The Great Uriel,
Banished Angel

LIFE MAKES ITS MOVES UNPREDICTABLY, DESIGNS ITS OWN PATH, and no matter how much we try to chart our course, life decides. We had proof of this on Sunday afternoon at three.

Ara, Ofelia, and I had agreed to meet at the asylum at that time. I was supposed to come in Harry's jeep, prepared to take the angel back to Galilea if Doña Ara insisted on the strict limits she had imposed before leaving him at the asylum. Anyway, Ofelia and I were going to suggest her son undergo systematic psychological and medical treatments for a few months. The truth is, I was actually no longer enthusiastic about this plan, and Ofelia perhaps even less so, but we both felt it would be only fair to leave the decision up to his mother.

I arrived a bit late, at about twenty past three, after being delayed at the hairdresser's, where I'd gone for an oil treatment, color highlights, and a trim.

When I arrived, Doña Ara wasn't yet there, and that was the first sign, although I did not realize it then, that fate was again running the show. Ofelia joined me, tapping her heels on the celebrated tiles—the ones that I said contained in their design the secret key to insanity—and from a distance I could detect a troubled look on her beautiful face.

"He's gone," she said.

"Who's gone?"

"The angel. Today at dawn or last night, he took off."

"How?"

"No one knows. Security is very good here. It's not easy to get out without authorization, in fact it's theoretically impossible. But he did it. At seven in the morning, a nurse's aide noticed his absence. There was a big commotion, and they looked for him everywhere, even on the roof. All to no avail, so we don't know where he is."

"It can't be! Oh, my God! Couldn't he be hiding somewhere, locked in a bathroom, under a bed, anything? We have to find him, Ofelia, no matter what! What are we going to tell his mother? That her son is lost again? The woman will die if she has to live through the same tragedy a second time."

"Calm down. You still have the jeep? Come on, let's go and look for him, he can't be very far. We already called the police and spent the whole morning searching for him, but on foot it's too slow. It'll be easier with the jeep."

"How come you didn't call me before? By now, heaven knows where he is or what may have happened to him; he's been wandering around for hours. Oh, my God, forgive me, it's all my fault, all my fault. Why is everything always my fault?"

"I learned about it around eight, and I came right away. I kept calling you, but—"

"You're right, damn it, I went out early biking. Let's get going, let's not waste any more time. Do you realize what this means?" I said, overwhelmed. "It'll be like finding a needle in a haystack . . . or a ring in the ocean. But you can do it, Ofelia!" I encouraged her, suddenly riding on a crest of wild optimism. "If you did it before, you can do it again."

We took off like two women possessed, beginning with the streets nearby and inquiring at every lunch counter, parking lot, tire shop, instant photo booth, hotel-by-the-hour, and food cart. We searched for him, risking our skins, even inside the ghastly drug dens on Cartucho Street. Whenever we saw a homeless person lying on the sidewalk under a heap of rags, we made sure it wasn't him.

The horrible grief I felt seemed insignificant when I thought of Ara's: during the seventeen years she searched for him, how often had she turned these same corners, gripped by an even greater anxiety, persevering but with an even more tattered hope.

During the nerve-racking search, I couldn't stop babbling all sorts of nonsense and telling myself over and over that this was an ominous day for me.

"As soon as I got up," I told Ofelia, "I went to feed Harry's canary, and guess what, it was dead."

"Dead?"

"Dead. Belly up in its cage, stiff as an old boot. Harry is going to think that I either didn't feed it or fed it too much. How embarrassing!"

"Buy him another one and switch them. He'll never notice."

"You think so?"

"All canaries look alike. Besides, stop worrying, this is actually a good omen. You throw the dead body into running water and forget about it. Nothing is unluckier than a caged canary."

My angel had vanished without a trace. The hungry city had swallowed him, wrapped him in its dirty blanket, and we didn't know how to get him back. What were the chances of survival for an angel of God in terrifying Bogotá, which gathers garbage on its street corners and anonymous corpses on its vacant lots? One in ten perhaps; perhaps only one in a hundred.

Around five in the afternoon, almost at my wit's end and about to admit defeat, I thought of one last, desperate plan: bring all the people down from Barrio Bajo, organize them in brigades, and have them search for the angel block by block, coordinating the operation from a general headquarters, which could be the asylum. Two or three hundred people could succeed where two could not.

Ofelia thought the whole thing was preposterous.

"That would be a herculean task," she protested, "like building the pyramids."

But since she had no alternative, we drove back to the asylum, looking for Ara in order to propose my emergency plan to her. We were almost there when I noticed, less than two hundred feet away, an unmistakable object of which there could only be one in the world: the royal blue velvet cape, trademark of Marujita de Peláez, flowing toward us on the shoulders of its owner.

"Miss Mona!" she shouted. "Thank heavens!"

"What happened?!"

All agitated, Marujita de Peláez ran so fast to meet us that she was out of breath and unable to speak.

"Tell us what happened, for heaven's sake!"

"The angel came back this morning! With a huge crowd following him!"

"The angel? Our angel? He got back safe and sound? How? When?"

"This morning, Miss Mona, around eleven. He looked glorious, like an apparition. And he didn't come alone, but with a crowd that kept growing larger, as more and more people followed him, glorifying and praising him."

"You mean to tell us that he walked all the way from the asylum to Galilea?"

"It seems so, Miss Mona. And those who came with him say he walked up through all those neighborhoods until he got up there, leading his many followers behind him."

"That's not possible!"

"Yes, miss, you heard me right, that's what happened. Part of the way he walked, and part of the way people carried him on their shoulders, some of them shouting 'Hail to the Angel of the Lord!' while the others answered 'Hail!' He seemed happy, as if he knew all the celebrating was in his honor. But since he did not come with you, Miss Mona, or with Dr. Ofelia, and because Doña Ara had an appointment with you at three, she sent me to tell you, in case you didn't know and were worried, that the angel was already home."

I hugged Ofelia and then Marujita, happy at the good news but upset with my angel, who had made me so miserable. I hugged Ofelia again, repeating, "See? Didn't I tell you? Don't you see that whenever he escapes, he returns home?"

I helped Marujita jump into the jeep.

"We're leaving now for Galilea," I announced. "Ofelia, are you coming?"

"Yes, let's go. Just give me a second to tell the asylum people to stop looking for him."

Contrary to what we had expected, we found Galilea completely deserted, in the way that only places jam-packed moments before can be. The neighborhood had sunk into a tense and eerie silence that blanketed everything like a thick coat of paint. Alley by alley we searched for the vanished multitudes, to no avail.

"Evidently, something very strange went on here," we said.

We saw some cops on armed patrol, watchful and keyed up, as if expecting to be struck on the back of the head by a sudden hail of stones. In front of us, a boy crossed the street like a shadow, holding his head with both hands, his face all bloody.

"Something horrible must have happened here . . ."

The soccer field, littered with rocks, broken bottles, and single shoes, was the center of destruction, an abandoned field of defeat.

"This is where they stood," Marujita de Peláez said, rubbing her eyes so they wouldn't play tricks on her. "I swear to God this is where I left them, the angel and all his followers."

We saw another group of cops crossing the grounds warily, as if afraid to make too much noise with their boots.

"I swear this is where I left them; it was a big crowd."

Seeing Galilea so deserted reminded me of the first day I came here. But it was worse now—without even the rain, only silence and fog, and the scared cops making it seem all the more ghostly.

A sergeant with a short mustache stopped us and asked for our IDs.

"Relocate your unit!" he ordered me.

"By unit you mean my car?" I asked.

"Affirmative. You have no business being out on the street. Didn't you hear about the curfew?"

"No, I didn't. I don't know what's going on. Could you please tell me what happened here?"

"Public disturbance. Now move, move, I told you to relocate your unit."

"Just a minute, I beg you. This lady lives in the neighborhood, and we are driving her home."

"Let her walk, and you get out of here."

"But she is ill, can't you see she's ill?"

The sergeant bent down to look in the backseat at Marujita de Peláez, who had put on her best throes-of-death expression.

"Then take her and get out, immediately."

"And at what time does the curfew start?"

"At seven sharp."

"Well, it's only a quarter past six; I still have another forty-five minutes."

I drove the jeep as close as I could to Barrio Bajo and parked. We had agreed that Ofelia and I would walk up to Ara's house and Marujita would meanwhile stay with the jeep in case a melee broke out again. I didn't want to return the car to Harry all burned up, or with spray-painted slogans like "Fatherland or Death," "Nupalom," "Bolivarian Militias," or anything of the sort. A destroyed car and a dead canary would have been too much punishment for Harry, who hadn't done anything.

The door of a house opened a fraction and a small woman looked out, sniffed the air like a mouse who wants to make sure the cat isn't around, saw the jeep and, recognizing Marujita de Peláez, came out cloaked in her shawl and a conspiratorial air.

"What are you doing out on the street, honey?" she quickly asked, opening her eyes wide. "Better hurry home, things are ugly here."

"We are going to Ara's house," Marujita answered.

"Don't go, it's risky, and nobody is there. They all fled up the mountain."

"What happened?" I blurted out, but the woman never heard me. She had already closed the door.

"Let's go," Ofelia said. "We can't do anything here. Let's go back to the city."

"Not yet." I was determined to get to the pink house, because I was sure I could find my angel there. I knew he was at the center of the turmoil, and I had decided to take him to my apartment, at least for a while, until the danger had passed.

"Don't do it," Ofelia warned me. "This situation isn't going to blow over in a day or two. And what are you going to do when you get over your infatuation?"

I responded with wounded heart that this was no fleeting infatuation, but the passion of my life. However, as I walked up the street through the deserted Barrio Bajo, abandoned even by the dogs, and where no windowpane had been spared in the scuffle, I felt more and more weighted down by my anguish, as if it were a huge burden on my shoulders. It's the overwhelming weight of this inconceivable love, I admitted to myself, and I wasn't sure how long I would be able to bear it.

When we got to Ara's house, the door was swinging open, blown back and forth by the wind.

"Ara? Doña Ara!"

Nobody answered, but it seemed we could hear light footsteps, like those of a child or a gnome.

"Orlando? Orlando!"

Nothing.

"In the name of God Almighty," Ofelia shouted in a theatrical voice, "if there's anybody there, identify yourself!"

No sound. Not even footsteps. We walked in through the

shadows, avoiding any dark, looming objects. We found only the smell of a cold stove and the silence of a turned-off radio.

Just as Marujita's acquaintance had warned us, there wasn't a soul around. The yard, the sink, Ara's cot, all once so meaningful to me, seemed suspended in the still air, frozen in time and useless, as if already resigned to oblivion.

"What about the footsteps?" Ofelia inquired. "If there is no one home, whose tiny steps did we hear?"

"Those were memories fleeing out the window," I answered, sensing at that precise moment that my brief but passionate story with the angel had come to an end, and that my long, dreary future without him had just begun. The loss tore at my insides, but I must confess that, at the same time, a furtive sense of relief refreshed my soul.

I groped my way to the trunk with the journals, which I had decided to appropriate. I had a right to them, I thought; they had been written for me and were the legacy of my love. I would keep them at my apartment until I could publish them; I would read them every night until I understood the meaning of every word.

My hands located the padlock, which was open, lifted the lid and searched inside, probing the dark space and finding nothing. Nothing. My hands searched again, covering every inch of the trunk's interior, with the same result: nothing.

Defeated, I sat down on the lid and tried to come to terms with reality: the trunk had been looted. A few blocks away, Father Benito was probably burning the fifty-three journals in an open fire; or the officer with the little mustache was cataloging and filing them as subversive material in some po-

lice archive. Then I gripped the cat-o'-nine-tails of my guilt
and started whipping myself: Why hadn't I taken them with
me before? I, and only I, could come across such a treasure
and do nothing to protect it, acting as if I could find another
at any turn.

Then it hit me: there were no journals anymore, I could
have made them up. They might have never existed. Nor
were there any people in the neighborhood, no angel, no
Orlando, no council. The characters and the events of the
past week had dissolved like the dazzling images captured
for an instant in a kaleidoscope.

We returned to Harry's jeep, but there too, the empti-
ness had preceded us like a phantom street sweeper. Marujita de Peláez had disappeared. Had she been frightened?
Had she rushed home to feed her pets? Had the police ab-
ducted her?

We called her name with timid voices that floated uphill
and returned to us, on their own echoes. We called again,
shouting at the top of our lungs. No one answered. We tried
to inquire at the home of the lady with the shawl, but nobody
came to the door. It was written that on that day Galilea
would remain closed and would not yield to me.

When we got to La Estrella I had lost all hope, knowing
full well that the erasing virus had wiped out the entire
episode. I was right. The store was closed and locked, hidden
behind its shuttered windows. I didn't knock; I wouldn't
have gotten any answer.

At that moment I noticed, on the floor of the jeep, the reflection of an intense blue. It was the velvet cape, the fragment that proved the truth of my mirage.

I stood in the middle of the street with the cape in my arms and felt relieved when it started to rain. I welcomed the drizzle that helped to dampen the embers of my anxiety. "Whatever the waters bring, the waters will wash away," I told myself, finding comfort in the empty resonance of that old saying.

Behind me was the city, spread out, silent, peaceful in the distance; in front of me, wrapped in dense strands of fog, the impenetrable mountain that might hide and shelter my angel, his people and his story, which, for an eternal week, had also been mine.

A wet wind blowing from the eucalyptus trees brought me a hint of peace and whispered a short message into my ear: "He is beyond your reach; it is no longer important whether you love him or he loves you."

I understood and agreed. The important thing was not to keep him close to me, but to set him free so he would be safe, so he could survive, so he might fulfill whatever purpose had brought him here, no matter how incomprehensible to me. I realized, without pain, that today was our day to say good-bye.

"Make haste, my beloved! And be like a gazelle or a young stag upon the mountains!" I would have liked to shout these words to him, the last words of the *Song of Songs,* which I had not heard since the days my Belgian grandfather read me the Scriptures, and which now came back to me.

Ofelia's voice brought me back to earth.

"We must do something," she said—words so often heard in this country, where, in the face of misfortune, there is nothing that can be done.

"What do you suggest?"

"I don't know, something. I'm worried about Doña Ara and her sons, who must be in trouble, but I'm also worried about you. You don't look so good."

"I'm all right. The circle is already closed for me. They, too, are all right. They know how to take care of themselves."

"Then let's get out of here before we get trapped by the curfew too."

"Yes, let's go."

But no week is ever canceled by decree, nor does it get erased from a lifetime like a text from a computer memory, least of all, the sacred and hallucinatory week that ended Sunday night. It can't be changed: Every moment of our lives leaves its mark.

Leaving marks on others as well as on me, my angel left the Galilea of his birth that Sunday to walk the region between the guerilla stronghold in the Cruz Verde plains and the quiet, warmer town of La Unión, inflaming and leading multitudes behind him. He vanished at the point where the Río Negro crosses the Río Blanco, in an unforgettable grand finale. According to some, his was a violent death at the hands of the military or paramilitary forces; according to even more, it was an ascension of body and soul to heaven.

Now that everything about him has been classified and

recorded, those seven months—that's how long his wanderings lasted—have been called his time of public life. This was the most glorious period of my angel's existence, and it coincided with the most difficult time of my pregnancy.

But to continue my tale in chronological order, I must return to the beginning of the end, to the night in Galilea when the curfew froze its streets, while the rest of the city continued its tame Sunday rhythm, as if nothing had happened.

I dropped Ofelia at her home and was returning to mine at the hour families usually have their after-dinner coffee and doze off in front of the television set. The traffic lights of Seventh Avenue were dutifully changing from green to amber to red, though the light traffic paid no attention to them, no matter what their color, when around 59th Street a sudden and terrible revelation tore me from the sentimental limbo I was lolling in. It was not true, as I had comfortably told myself a short time earlier, that I had serenely decided to forget my love. The truth was a hundred and eighty degrees in the opposite direction, because it was he who had abandoned me. Contrary to all appearances, neither I nor Crucifija, nor the D.T.F.A., nor anybody had any control over the angel. He did not belong to any of us, not even to Ara. He did not need us. We, each in our own way, had clung on to him. Though it hurt, it was clear that his destiny was not, nor had it ever been, in my hands. His fate on earth was known only to him; the road he traveled did not lead to me as a goal, nor was it even within the influence of my wishes.

I pondered further and started to doubt what I had taken for granted before: that at some point he had loved me or felt some affection for me; even that he had truly been aware of my existence; or that in the frailty of his memory there still lingered some image of me.

With this sudden change in perception, I switched roles from that of deserter to that of deserted, from perpetrator to victim, and it made me feel a wrenching and bitter resentment.

I started torturing myself with thoughts of how to win him back, how to prevent his flight—an absurd notion considering that only moments earlier, I had accepted the disappearance of the whole episode with some relief.

But things were not that simple, they never are, because in life, like it or not, the law of unforeseen consequences inevitably governs. When I got home a few minutes later, sitting by the entrance of my building was none other than Orlando, his eyes drowsy from a long wait. With him, the missing evidence of my love story reappeared, and reality, momentarily interrupted, resumed its course.

It so happened that around noon Doña Ara had sent Orlando to stay with me while she and the angel were forced to run away and hide in the mountain. Orlando had been waiting for my return, sitting on the granite steps, with the infinite patience and immobility of a saintly stylite, which the poor learn to do early in childhood.

But Orlando hadn't come alone. He had brought with him a heavy sack that I first thought contained his clothes but actually held his mother's journals. All fifty-three of the Norma notebooks with the angel's dictations intact, saved from disaster and now miraculously placed in my hands. Father Benito had not burned them, and the officer with the mustache had not confiscated them: Ara herself had sent them to me with the idea that in my home they would be safe. I hugged those journals with a fervor reserved for saints' relics or the last splinter recovered from Christ's cross. Even though I had lost my angel, I now owned his voice for the first time. And now that I think of it, I realize that this was the first time, but hardly the last, that I would cling to the written word and let life pass me by. Perhaps these were the first signs of weariness that marked the end of my youth.

There was nothing in my refrigerator but a few somewhat greenish-looking sausages that I camouflaged as hot dogs. Orlando wolfed them down while reporting, in his best torrential style, the events of that afternoon. He was describing many things at the same time, reinforcing his words with the appropriate sound effects, his eyes wide awake and sparkling. Often I had to make him repeat himself in order to find the connections in his frenzied outpouring. He started with the story of the angel's arrival in the neighborhood, which I had already heard from Marujita.

"Marujita de Peláez already told me that part," I told him.

"Then, where do you want me to start?"

"I know how the angel appeared, but I don't know how he disappeared."

"So you want me to tell you about the soccer field?"

"Right."

"Well, as the angel followers were filling the court, *whammo!,* that's when it happened! They had a rumble with Father Benito's rabble and those guys from the D.T.F.A., who were the meanest ones, see, and really set on not letting them go through."

"That's not surprising . . ."

"And my mother was getting desperate, moaning 'Oh, my son, the D.T.F.A. boys are going to kill him! Leave him alone, he is innocent!' But the D.T.F.A. guys did not buy it, and just got fiercer."

"Did they hurt him? Tell me, did they hurt the angel?" I asked, but Orlando ignored my interruptions.

"And when we were getting ready for the worst, *tan-ta-rah!* Sweet Baby Killer appeared, elbowing her way through the squabble; she beat up the D.T.F.A. guys, lifted the angel onto her shoulders and, kicking and hitting, got him out of there: *Wham! Pow! Whack!* Take this one, and that one! She would hit anybody in her way, see, and so she brought him home safe and sound, without a scratch."

"Then why didn't all of you stay there? Why did you go up the mountain?" I needed him to give me some convincing reasons to counter my disappointment and restore my hopes. "Why did you?"

"Because before we knew it, the damn cops had taken over our neighborhood, see, a hundred, maybe a thousand cops with nightsticks trying to break up the group. *Crack! Whack!* One man was hit on the head. *Aagh!* And the D.T.F.A. guys, who are really chicken, ran away and hid inside the church while we, the angel people, fought back, went up the mountain, and took our stand at the Bethel Grottoes, which, as you know, are like an underground fortress."

"Who took a stand at the grottoes?"

"Why, all of us from Barrio Bajo."

"And did you have an encounter with the police?"

"Of course we did. You should have seen the shower of stones, it was sensational; too bad you missed it, Monita. We even set tires on fire and rolled them down."

"And the angel? What was the angel doing?"

"Nothing. He didn't take part in this. But then there was a panic, someone started shouting. First it was only one person, but then everybody was shouting."

"What were you shouting?"

"We were shouting 'Break it up, the cops have gas! We'll suffocate in the grottoes!'"

"And what did you do?"

"We began getting out through the openings at the back of the grottoes and spread out over the mountain, and there the cops didn't have a chance, they really lost out, because we hid in the mountain, where not even the Devil could find us."

"And the angel? What was happening to Doña Ara and the angel?"

"Nothing. I told you."

"But where were they?"

"They were in the mountain, and probably still are, with all the others from Barrio Bajo."

"I don't understand. When the stone throwing stopped, why didn't they go back to their homes?"

"Are you crazy? Don't you know the cops are vengeful and never forgive? But mostly we didn't return because we heard what was happening at La Estrella."

The following day, after attending an editors' committee meeting, I took an assignment to interview a former drug trafficker now financing a clinic for addicts, after which I rushed to Galilea on my last trip with the jeep. Harry was due back that afternoon.

I found that real life was slowly returning to its normal pace. The owner of La Estrella was again behind the counter, and I wanted to personally verify the contents of the message Ara had received from there. I assumed it was not quite as dramatic as hyperbolic Orlando reported, telling of juvenile delinquents and an unstoppable conspiracy by Father Benito and the D.T.F.A. to kill the angel.

I learned that immediately after the stone-throwing incident, six of the D.T.F.A. boys had shown up at La Estrella and were drinking beer, counting their money, and boasting that they had kicked the angel and his followers out of the neighborhood and would not let them return: "It is time for that little angel to go back to heaven."

Witnesses had taken this as a death threat, and putting two and two together, they figured out that Father Benito had contracted the D.T.F.A. gang to get rid of the angel, as well as to ensure that the exile of the rest of the priest's opponents would be permanent. This version was pretty close to Orlando's.

It was at this point that the story started to become a legend. Or that, for me, it changed from a short and dizzying succession of events into monotonous and prolonged nostalgia.

I remember well that Monday, at La Estrella, the day after the angel fled to the mountain, the day I made the decision to go after him, to track him down, to follow him to the end of the world. I would give up everything, I would plunge into the void so as not to lose him. I remember that I was moved by anger and wounded pride, emotions more powerful than love, but also more deceptive. I can't remember, however, the labyrinth of postponements and pretexts—all so banal and insignificant—work permits, upset stomachs, roads closed by guerrillas, lack of money to leave with my aunt to pay the rent—all the twists and turns that caused my resolve to falter.

The truth is, by the time the definitive obstacle made its appearance, I had become so entangled in the demanding, petty affairs of everyday life that I had already let the love of my life escape. This is clear to me now, though I did not realize it then. My backpack was full and ready for the great journey on the day that a piece of paper, which turned violet in contact with my urine, gave me the stark news that I was pregnant.

I felt awful at the beginning, throwing up so often that I seemed more possessed by the devil than pregnant. I cried my days away, my boss got suspicious, my breasts started swelling, and Ofelia scolded me for having made love without taking precautions.

"Better forget what I said," she told me a few days later.

"It's not your fault. After all, who would think of asking an angel to wear a condom?"

Once in a while, between bouts of crying and throwing up, I heard news about the wanderings of the baby's father. The reports came from his Barrio Bajo followers, converted into an army of hungry, unarmed, ragged people, who slept in hideouts and caves, like birds in the forest, ate whatever they could find until they gradually began returning in small groups. The more daring returned first; next those who had been less involved with the angel and therefore had less to fear from the D.T.F.A.; and finally, those who, defeated by the uncertainties of nomadic life, decided that it was worth risking the perils of their neighborhood to be able to return to their homes.

First they told me simple stories: that the angel had eaten green guavas at the exit of Punta del Zorro, or goat's meat at a food stand at Choachí Square. Stories such as the one about his taming an angry bull in a corral at Miguelito Salas' hacienda were easily believable.

But as the circle of listeners expanded, they began to speak of him in less personal and more mythological terms, as if they were talking about Superman or drug czar Pablo Escobar. Amazing feats were recounted. They claimed his body, naked, could stand the cold of the plains, never knowing hunger or exhaustion. His sweetness filled the valleys, his radiance lit up the roads, his steps left behind a trail of stars.

More than once I received fairly accurate information on his whereabouts. I was still burning with anxiety and the desire to be with him, but such a possibility became increasingly remote because the baby, in spite of my violent psycho-somatic reaction, had settled inside of me with such amazing self-assurance and such unconditional trust that I could not, even for a moment, consider endangering my pregnancy. Without being aware of it, I got involved in the cozy domestic routine of knitting little smocks, taking iron and calcium pills, and painting walls sky blue, preparations that were entirely incompatible with exhausting nightly pilgrimages over mountain ridges in heavy downpours.

Soon total strangers started to tell me about his extraordinary deeds, men and women who swore they had witnessed the presence of the angel in all his glory. For the first time I began hearing about his miracles: he had saved the town of Santa María de Arenales from a flood, he had caused manna from heaven to rain on the starving village of Remolinos. Some of the acts credited to him were ambiguous and hard to interpret, such as when, according to friendly sources, he had punished an adulterous woman by leaving a glowing mark on her forehead, or when on a sunny Sunday, he blinded some peasants who were looking at him in ecstasy. This only increased his prestige because, in the innocent eyes of believers, it is no more miraculous for a blind person to be able to see than for a seeing person to go blind.

Surprising as it might seem, of the totally dedicated councilwomen, the first one to abandon him was the one who loved him most: Ara.

"I came for Orlando," she confessed to me one day in a deeply pained voice, "to take care of him the way

God intended. By following a son who has never been mine, I am abandoning the one who has always been there for me."

Sweet Baby Killer was next; she had taken care of the angel faithfully, with humble devotion and the most doglike loyalty, until an injury in her leg became infected, then gangrenous, and finally turned into a fetid and wormy sore, making it physically impossible for her to continue following him.

As for Sister María Crucifija, it was said that she had taken advantage of the absence of the other councilwomen to take charge of the angel and exploit his public image to her own benefit; that she had become an uncompromising and dogmatic leader, as domineering and as manipulative of the unofficial story as Father Benito had been of the official truth. She was said to harangue her followers, in the name of the angel, with contradictory oratory: grandiose as well as ridiculous, violent but purely rhetorical.

And yet, despite the awful notoriety that soon surrounded her, which is still associated with her name, I must admit that Sister María Crucifija carried out her mission. Every angel must have a prophet on earth to announce and interpret him to lowly humans; just as Yahweh had Christ and Allah had Mohammed, the Angel of Galilea had María Crucifija. It is clear that my angel never aspired to renown, and it is quite probable that, without María Crucifija, he would have in fact remained obscure.

It was Crucifija's fate to disappear from his story after the F.A.R.C. Thirteenth Front, the dominant guerrilla group in the area, stripped her of authority and gave the angel the honorary title of commander in chief, dragging him along in order to soften the hearts of the peasants and open new areas for the rebels' proselytizing activities.

But not even the guerrillas were able to hold him for long. He found a way to leave them behind and go on, always alone, always farther, never looking back or stopping to rest, urged on by his supernatural strength, and guided by the star of his mysterious destiny.

On one occasion, when my pregnancy was close to term, Doña Ara heard that her son and his followers were encamped near a trail in the foothills known as Fuente Leones, God knows why. It so happened that an uncle of mine owned a nearby hacienda and let us have it for the night, so we decided to visit the angel.

We managed to see him, more mature and stronger than before, but more isolated than ever, in the midst of a dramatic, rocky landscape with emerald green vegetation, violet clouds, and purple shadows. We saw him only at a distance; we were separated by a compact and agitated mass of followers who would not let us get any closer. Not that we would have wanted to, even if we could have. We did not wish to interrupt the intensity of his mystic trance: head high and tense, he stood on a sharp stone outcropping, his magnificent body leaning dangerously toward the abyss, deaf to adulation, oblivious of his worshipers, his own divine nature alien to power and glory, his raven locks surrendered to the wind, his gaze lost in the sunset glow.

I can't deny that when I saw him, the flames started to leap again in my heart. But I did not take a single step toward him, not one. *Noli me tangere* was the defiant and imperative shout from his silent lips, his unfocused eyes, his entire being. And I understood his message: Do not desire to touch me. And even though I was dying inside, I knew to obey.

I never saw him again. Shortly afterward, there were certain events, for which there was never an explanation, that determined his disappearance at the place where Río Blanco and Río Negro converge. Today a primitive stone shrine, erected in his honor, marks the spot.

You are awake in the dark on a quiet September evening. You are silent, listening intently. Can you hear anything? A rush of wings, a gentle rustle of feathers . . . A slight flutter that barely shifts the breeze . . . That is my voice.

Do you feel an inner glow, so delicate it hardly warms the center of your being? It is my presence, rarefied by space and distance, that breaks through oblivion and reaches you. Coming from the shadows of the banished, the fallen angel speaks to you. I have come to whisper into your ear the heroic deeds of my ancient battles.

I am what is left of Archangel Uriel, former flame of God, fierce conflagration that in his glorious past warmed and brightened planets and hearts. It was I who maintained the balance of galaxies, the universes already created and those yet to be created. I was the one, and no other, who roamed the blue plains meditating on the order of the universe, now destroyed and subject to the vagaries of a crazy fate. It was on me that all creatures born under the sign of Libra used to depend; my steps echoed over the southern hemisphere, now deprived of my guidance and open to the calamities of plague, famine, and war. My retinue consisted of ten men wise in the art of science who kept to themselves, always remembering what is so often forgotten, that true science is knowing that you know not.

You see me reduced to an essence that is almost extinct: I am the embers breathing under the ashes. I survive in hiding, anonymous, in the fervor of the ignorant masses, so wise that they offer their praise to the angels, without even knowing their names.

You ask yourself what became of my former grandeur. Who extinguished the light that shone forth with such intensity, who tarnished my pale star, who darkened my translucent alabaster skin and cut off the locks that fell over my shoulders. You want to know when my wars began.

It happened when men resented the aloofness of God, cloistered and inaccessible as Supreme Monarch of the high heavens, and sought the protection of angels, present at every corner of the Earth, participating in the nature of all things, even the smallest, such as mice and sewing needles. Every man and every woman could trust a winged friend, and from the first breath of air, every newborn felt the breath of a guardian angel over every cradle. And all countries, even those not on maps, every city, every river, brook, mountain, and lake, all had their guiding angels. There was no human endeavor without a benefactor. One for masons, another for shepherds, one for the ruler and an equal one for the vassal, for the nobleman as well as the serf, for the musician and for the circus acrobat, for the knight and also for his squire, for the deer hunter, the vintner woman, the marchioness, the goat milker, the woman giving birth, the baker's wife.

It happened that during the seraphic reign on Earth, I, Uriel, had my place next to Michael, Gabriel, and Raphael in the council of the major archangels, equal in hierarchy and at the same distance from the throne: in the North Raphael, the pilgrim patron of travelers and foreigners, bearer of the name of God engraved on a tablet on his chest, healer of illnesses and injuries. In the East Michael, beardless and fiery warrior, whose war cry is "Who is like God!" and whose enemy, the Dragon, falls beheaded by a single swish of his sword. In the West Gabriel, the messenger, clothed in magnificent vestments, known with great admiration as universal bearer of good news, in the Bible as well as in the Koran. And in the South I, Uriel, thinker and fire-lover. The great Uriel, flame of God, in whom Enoch, the antediluvian patriarch wrongly considered apocryphal, recognized the highest point in the heavens, lower only than the Father.

The host of angels that came down to Earth with me was welcomed by humble and simple souls, which for others was cause for alarm and discontent; there were those who were terrified to see our power over all beings and all things. "Pagan pantheism!" shouted the high dignitaries of the Church, corroded by jealousy because they felt displaced. "Heretical animism!" exclaimed the doctors of divinity, inquisitorial and distrustful, feeling the threat to the preeminence of Jesus, Son of God.

On me, Uriel, then called The Great, fell the wrath of Pope Zacharias, who, carried away by ill will, forbade the utterance of my name and condemned my followers to the stake.

But anathema and punishment only served to fan the flames, and the faith in me spread over the Holy Roman Empire, and even beyond, like wildfire in the dry summer forests. At the same time, the number of my enemies multiplied, some very powerful ones among them, such as Boniface, saint and martyr, and the sovereigns Charles the Great and Pepin the Short.

One adversity upon another befell me. The council of Laodicea, the Soissons synod, the German council, all decided to prevail over me, recognizing as authentic angel names only those three mentioned in the Scriptures, namely, Gabriel, Raphael, and Michael, and consequently ruled that all others were names of demons—mine, Uriel, being one of them. My name was therefore removed from the council of the four angels, and placed at the head of the banished, followed by Raguel, Jubuel, Jonia, Adimus, Tubuas, Sabaot, Simiel, Jejodiel, Sealtiel, and Baraquiel.

Whoever invoked these angels, or others of unknown names, was declared superstitious, and was excommunicated and condemned to death.

Michael, Raphael, and Gabriel were the only three who retained their titles and honors, while I, the fourth among the great, was now at the head of the proscribed hordes. Pope Clement III ordered my likeness removed from the Santa Maria degli Angeli in Rome, and his example was soon followed by bishops and abbots, so that on mosaics and frescoes I was reduced to an anonymous blotch of stucco, next to the recognized and eternal grandeur of Michael, of Gabriel, and of Raphael.

The theologian Gioseppe de Turre tried to justify these out-

rages, pointing out the danger that would result if any of the faithful could make up odd names for angels out of their own free will.

What Gioseppe de Turre and the other theologians really feared was the loss of authority and command over people's beliefs. They also feared that we, the Lord's angels, being almost as perfect as the Lord himself, almost as endowed with beauty, power, and attributes, might equal Him or even rise above Him.

Driven by their hatreds and their fears, the Church hierarchy persecuted those deemed idolatrous until forests and commons in the south of France turned red. In the Lico Valley they burned crosses and tore down shrines built in my honor. Hundreds of my followers were burned at the stake; they died while still shouting "Non moritur Uriel!"

But I endure, despite everything. Fire and bloodshed could not eradicate me from the Earth. I survive, like embers glowing under the ashes, in the smallest of relics that flouted the censors, and which today speak to the initiate of my passing through this world.

I am mentioned in Saint Ambrosio's hymn, who used to pray to the winds "Non moritur, Gabriel, non moritur, Raphael, non moritur, Uriel."

In a lead plate with a prayer to drive away malignant tumors, found near Arkenise.

Among the Copts, who still celebrate my feast every fifteenth of July.

In the Canon Universalis of the Ethiopians.

In Oriental calendars.

In litanies and medieval exorcisms disseminated in Syria, Pisidia, and *Phrygia*, of which isolated fragments have been found.

As a warrior with Oriental features you can find me in the golden shadows of the Capella Palatina in Palermo.

I am in Sopó, soft of body, courtier in bearing, ambiguous in my gaze, in a colonial oil painting whose anonymous creator wanted to clothe me in velvet and place a flaming sword in my right hand.

My life is evanescent, diffused, almost vanished, in these manuscript pages, in which you, woman of Galilea, have tried to sustain the agonizing throbbing of my blood.

I therefore endure in you, and to you I turn in the quiet stillness of September. Not much is left of me, but I am here. I will be the propitious shadow that will frequent your days; the spring waters that will soothe you in your hours of fear; a faithful dog, always at your side, along the road; the arrow that will show you the way when it is time for you to depart.

Kneel, woman. Open your arms like branches of a tree. Make room in your house and open the window, so that whatever is left of this archangel, who is fleeing in fright, may enter without fear and find refuge, where he may glow, secretly and discreetly, like a will-o'-the-wisp.

Repeat Ambrosio's litany with me and save me from oblivion: Non moritur Uriel! Non moritur Uriel! Non moritur Uriel!

Manuel,
Son of Woman

ONCE A WEEK I GO UP TO GALILEA, TO BE WITH DOÑA ARA AND to take my daughter, who is already six, to visit.

Orlando, her uncle Orlando, has a day job as a graphic artist at *Somos* and goes to school nights for his technical secondary education. He is still as intense as ever, and of so much help to me that I don't know what I would do without him.

Sister María Crucifija ended up in Belén de Umbría, a coffee plantation town. She is said to have become a hermit, spending her solitary days and nights on the mountains in a dismal wild beast's den. We learned that Sweet Baby Killer lost her leg and is wearing a wooden prosthesis, which does not prevent her from making a living as a stevedore in the port of Buenaventura. Marujita de Peláez still lives in Galilea but no longer dons a blue cape, nor a cape of any color, for that matter. Father Benito died a few years ago, not of lung cancer, as might have been expected in view of his Lucky Strike habit, but from a heart attack after all his tantrums.

The D.T.F.A. dissolved because most of its members went to Medellín, to swell the ranks of the drug peddlers.

From the day I took Lovely Ofelia to visit the Muñís sisters, they have become her primary gurus. The two old ladies love her and concoct ointments to preserve her doll's skin forever, and for her part, Ofelia sees them frequently and makes no decisions in her love life without their advice.

Doña Ara makes a living by crocheting bedspreads and tablecloths. She has a serene life, taking care of Orlando and bestowing upon her granddaughter—my daughter—all the love that she was unable to give her older son when he was a child. She has not heard from him since he vanished, and has not even received further dictations from him; therefore, she considers her job as his chronicler completed.

She will not allow me to publish the fifty-three journals until after her death, with the exception of the six fragments that, after much pleading, I was able to include in the present volume. She was even less inclined to give them to the Church, though the Archbishop of Santafé de Bogotá went all the way up to her home to claim them himself. Doña Ara doesn't live in the same house; she has moved to another one seven blocks down.

Her former home has become a shrine, so popular that even presidential candidates visit it on the campaign trail.

Along the old Barrio Bajo Street there are now wide cement stairs leading all the way up, with small stands on both sides selling medallions, religious cards, prayers, and all kinds of mementos of the Angel of Galilea, who is accepted nowadays by sextons, bishops, and other members of the ecclesiastical hierarchies. Most popular are relics containing bits of his actual mantle and of leather from his sandals. False relics and fake mementos from someone who in his lifetime had neither shirt nor shoes.

The cement stairs end at the massive, new basilica, built over what was known as Bethel. Below, among the remains of the grottoes and within the basilica's foundations, dwells an underground army of beggars, drug addicts, and homeless kids who live off the coins that pilgrims throw them. There are other new developments, such as a bus terminal to transport visitors, and a couple of guesthouses to provide lodging for those who come from afar.

The Basilica of the Holy Angel is its name, and next to the main altar one can see a plaster statue of a white, blond boy with a pair of gigantic wings that help him alight from the heavens. He wears a short Roman toga, a crimson mantle, a fake gold crown, and crushes under his foot—which is shod in a Greek sandal—a vile beast, without any apparent disgust. Behind the statue an electronic strip, like the ones used to advertise McDonald's hamburger prices, spells out letter by letter in tiny red lights all of the ten commandments, the seven sacraments, and the acts of mercy.

That impressive production set has nothing to do with us, and the angel so venerated by them is not our angel. Doña Ara, Crucifija, the child, and I do not fit in the official story they have created for him, and neither does Sweet Baby Killer or Marujita de Peláez. The new parish priest likes only heavenly, gilded stories and wants to hear nothing from anyone who would tie the Angel of Galilea to this earth. And, least of all, if it involves women. To believe in the angel, the Church had to get rid of his affections, his flesh and his bones, and convert him into a legend of their own devising.

Otherwise, the neighborhood has not changed much. Except for La Estrella, which has new owners and is no longer called a store, but a supermarket. There is still no pavement and no sewer system, and in winter, every now and then, the rains carry away a house.

I'm still working for *Somos.* I'm still writing the same banalities, but now I get paid more for them. I live with my daughter, and my life is devoted almost entirely to her. I did not want to get married, and although since her birth several men have been part of my life, I still yearn for my angel, mostly quietly, but at times such as now, with a vehemence that I find overwhelming.

I can never thank the people of Galilea enough for opening my eyes to what I would not have seen otherwise. It is hard to spot an angel and, without help, I would have been like many others, who were close to him but never knew it.

The place where my daughter feels really at home is Galilea. With Orlando and a cooking pot, she hikes up the mountain to prepare play food on an open fire; she plays and fights with the other children on the street, and sometimes disappears for hours until I find her asleep in front of a neighbor's TV. Luckily, the neighborhood people treat her as just another child. But at the beginning it was different.

When she was about to be born, at least fifty or sixty people, bearing candles and flowers, assembled at the maternity ward of the National Clinic. The others waited expectantly up there in the neighborhood. They claimed that all the favorable signs had appeared: the right number of stars in the heavens, the blackbird's song at the prescribed time, the precise formation of sediment at the bottoms of their coffee cups.

It was a truly exuberant commotion, and the doctors and nurses didn't have a clue as to what was going on. But I did, and was deeply distressed. What the people were expecting was the fulfillment of the prophecy, the new link in the chain, the birth of an angel, the son of an angel, the continuation of a tradition centuries old that had to be projected into the future.

I had made a decision: I would take my baby far away to another city, where it could grow up without the weight of such a stigma hanging over its head. Of course, I felt infinitely relieved when I found out it was a girl. But the news hit the people of Galilea like a stroke of lightning on a frozen bucket of water. It meant the reincarnation had not taken place: a female angel was inconceivable to them.

Their disappointment was extreme, and the people quickly forgot about the girl, as well as me. Well, they didn't really forget us, because they love and accept us. Let's say rather that all past events and the girl's origin have been fortunately consigned to oblivion.

She herself knows little of all this. All I told her was that her father was an exceptional being, and that his name was Manuel. How do I know his name was Manuel? The Muñís sisters told me. It seems that the angel's grandfather, besides being a despicable man, was also a religious fanatic and, before selling the boy to the foreign couple, had him baptized to ease his conscience. Manuel is the name he gave him. That's what the Muñís sisters said, or rather Chofa did—Rufa still doesn't say a word—and I chose to believe her. First because Manuel means "The One Who Is with Us." And second, because in the end it really made no sense to tell the girl, taking into account the vagaries of life, that her father had no name.

It is a blessing that my girl can grow up under ordinary circumstances, just as she is, a normal, healthy child. For me, of course, she is a miracle child, but that is understandable, since I am her mother. Doña Ara sees her with grandmother's eyes every time she mumbles "This little girl is a bright sun!" I have never noticed any unusual qualities in her that would set her apart from others. She adores her uncle Orlando more than anybody in the world, collects comic books, hates vegetables, uses a calculator for her arithmetic homework, dresses her dolls, and is obsessed with Nintendo. Although I baptized her Damaris, my mother's name, we really don't call her Damaris; it doesn't seem to fit her, and everybody has a different nickname for her. She is very beautiful, I have to admit, but not more so than many other children.

Only one thing makes me feel uneasy about her. It's something that keeps me awake nights and makes me worry: the profound perceptiveness of her dark eyes, which understand everything without the need of words, and which, nevertheless, sometimes make you believe they are looking at you when they are not.

About the Author

LAURA RESTREPO was born in Colombia in 1950. She has a degree in the liberal arts from the Universidad de los Andes in Bogotá and postgraduate qualifications in political science at the same university. She was a professor of literature at the National University, Colombia, before going into politics and later into journalism. She has been publisher of the weekly magazine *Semana*. In 1984 she was a member of the Peace Commission that brought the Colombian government and the guerrillas to the negotiating table.

Among her many Spanish language novels are *La isla de la pasión* (*Island of Passion*) and *El leopardo al sol* (*Leopard in the Sun*). She has also written a children's novel, *Las vacas comen espaguetis* (*Cows Eat Spaghetti*). Laura Restrepo lives in Bogotá.